"I will find the baby." And he'd put away whoever had taken the child.

He escorted her through the back to a holding cell. Ryder scanned the space as he followed. Two cells. The other was empty.

At least she wasn't being thrown in with some dangerous derelict.

The cell door closed with a clang. Tia looked small and helpless inside that cell, yet he'd seen the fight in her when she'd confronted her ex.

"Please find Jordie," she whispered in a raw, pained voice. "He's just a few days old. He…needs me."

Yes, he did.

But Ryder had seen the worst of society on that last case. The head of the ring had seemed like an upstanding citizen. But evil had lurked beneath the surface.

Did Tia deserve to have her son back?

For the life of him, he wanted to believe her. Maybe because no kid should grow up thinking his mother had gotten rid of him, like he had.

The Last McCullen

RITA HERRON

First Published in Great Britain 2017
By Mills & Boon, an imprint of HarperCollins*Publishers*
1 London Bridge Street, London, SE1 9GF

Large Print edition 2017

ISBN: 978-0-263-07232-7

Our policy is to use papers that are natural, renewable and recyclable products and made from wood grown in sustainable forests. The logging and manufacturing processes conform to the legal environmental regulations of the country of origin.

Printed and bound in Great Britain
by CPI Antony Rowe, Chippenham, Wiltshire

USA TODAY bestselling author **Rita Herron** wrote her first book when she was twelve but didn't think real people grew up to be writers. Now she writes so she doesn't have to get a real job. A former kindergarten teacher and workshop leader, she traded storytelling to kids for writing romance, and now she writes romantic comedies and romantic suspense. Rita lives in Georgia with her family. She loves to hear from readers, so please visit her website, www.ritaherron.com.

This one is for all the fans of
The Heroes of Horseshoe Creek series
who wrote asking for the twins' stories!

Chapter One

Ryder Banks needed a shower, a cold beer and some serious shut-eye.

Three months of deep undercover work had paid off, though. He'd caught the son-of-a-bitch ringleader of a human trafficking group who'd been kidnapping and selling teenage girls as sex slaves.

Sick bastard.

He scrubbed a hand over his bleary eyes as he let himself inside his cabin. The musty odor and the dust motes floating in the stale air testified to the fact that he hadn't seen this place in months.

Tired but still wired from the arrest, he grabbed

a beer from the fridge, kicked off his shoes and flipped on the news.

"This is Sheriff Maddox McCullen of Pistol Whip, Wyoming." The newscaster gestured toward a tall, broad-shouldered man with dark hair. "Sheriff McCullen has just arrested the person responsible for three-year-old Tyler Elmore's abduction and for the murder of the boy's mother, Sondra Elmore. Sheriff?"

"The man we arrested was Jim Jasper, a sheriff himself," Sheriff McCullen said. "He confessed to the homicide."

"What about the man who was originally charged with the murder?" The news anchor consulted his notes. "Cash Koker, wasn't that his name?"

McCullen nodded. "Sheriff Jasper also admitted that he framed Koker, so Koker has been cleared of all charges." Sheriff McCullen offered a smile. "On a more personal note, my brothers and I learned that Mr. Koker—Cash—

is our brother. He and his twin were kidnapped at birth from our family."

"That explains the reason his last name isn't McCullen?"

"Yes, he was given the name of the foster parent who first took him in." McCullen paused. "We're delighted to reconnect with him. We're also searching for Cash's twin. We hope he'll come forward if he's watching."

A photo of Cash Koker flashed onto the screen.

Ryder swallowed hard. Dammit, the man not only resembled the other McCullen brothers with his dark hair, square jaw, big broad shoulders and rugged build, but he looked just like *him*.

The number for the sheriff's office flashed onto the screen and Ryder cursed, then hit the off button for the TV.

Maddox McCullen was a damn good actor. The emotions on his face seemed real.

He wanted the world to believe that his twin brothers had been stolen from his family.

But that was a lie.

Ryder knew the truth.

The McCullens had sold those babies.

All for the money to expand their ranch, Horseshoe Creek.

Sure, on the surface, the McCullens looked like model citizens, like a loving family. But that family had dirty little secrets.

Although he'd always known he was adopted, and that his adopted parents, Myra and Troy Banks, loved him, four years ago after Troy died, he'd had a bug to find his birth parents. A little research had led him to the McCullens.

He'd confronted his mother, and she'd broken down and admitted that she'd gotten him through a private adoption. That his birth parents had needed money at the time. She and Troy had wanted a child so badly they'd paid to get custody of Ryder.

A hundred thousand dollars. That's what he'd been worth.

The Bankses had sacrificed their entire life

savings to take him in while the McCullens used the cash to buy more cattle and horses.

But they hadn't told him about Cash. Did his parents know he had a twin?

If so, why hadn't they adopted both of them?

Because they couldn't afford it…

So where had Cash been all these years?

His phone buzzed, and he glanced at the number. His boss, Connor Statham, assistant director of the FBI's criminal investigative division.

He pressed Connect. "Ryder."

"Listen, Banks, I know you just came off a major case, but I need you on another one."

The shower beckoned. So did a bottle of bourbon to stave off the anger eating at him over that news report.

"It's a missing baby and possible homicide—mother insists someone kidnapped her infant. Soon-to-be ex-husband suggested the mother did something with the child. She thinks *he* did something to the baby."

Ryder's stomach knotted. "She thinks he killed his own child?"

A tense heartbeat passed. "Either that or he sold him."

Statham's statement echoed in Ryder's head as if someone had hit him in the skull with a sledgehammer. The situation hit too close to home. "You think she's telling the truth?"

"He said, she said. Local deputy who took her statement thinks she's unstable. He issued an Amber Alert, but so far nothing's come of it."

Anger slammed into Ryder. What kind of world was it that people sold their children?

"I want you to investigate, watch her," Statham said. "If she's lying and gave the baby to someone or hurt the child, she'll slip up."

Ryder downed another sip of his beer. "Text me her name and where she lives." A second later, the name Tia Jeffries appeared on his screen along with an address.

He hurried to the shower. The bourbon would have to wait. So would the sleep.

If this woman had hurt her baby, she wouldn't get away with it. And if the father was at fault, he'd throw him in jail and make sure he never saw the light of day again.

TIA JEFFRIES SLIPPED the Saturday night special from her purse as she parked her minivan outside her ex-husband's apartment. A low light burned in the bedroom, the outline of a man—Darren—appearing in front of the window.

A woman sidled up behind him, hands reaching around Darren's naked midriff, her fingers trailing lower to stroke his erection.

Bile rose to Tia's throat. How many times had she fallen prey to the man's charms and jumped into bed with him?

Only she'd believed he was marriage material at the time. Father material for the child she'd always wanted.

A baby that would be the beginning of the big family she'd dreamed about having.

The one that would replace the family she'd lost years ago.

Her mother, father and brother were all wiped out in a plane crash when they were on the way to her college graduation.

Her fault.

She would never forgive herself.

If she hadn't insisted on them attending, they would still be alive.

But the loss of her baby boy, Jordan, was even worse.

Only Jordan wasn't dead. At least, she didn't believe he was.

Someone had stolen him from her bedroom while she'd been sleeping. The police had questioned her as if she'd done something with him.

Guilt made her throat clog with tears. She certainly hadn't hurt Jordan. But she was supposed to protect him. Keep him safe.

Instead she'd been sleeping while he disappeared.

She'd begged the police to find her baby. Had told them that she suspected Darren.

But they hadn't believed her. Darren was a good old boy. Tight with the mayor's wife, because he could charm the pants off anyone.

But Darren had lied.

And Tia was going to find out the reason.

Her hands shook as she gripped the handle of the .33. Sweat beaded on her neck and forehead.

The bedroom excitement heated up, Darren and the woman moving together in a frenzied, harried coupling. Sickened at the sight, she closed her eyes to shut out the images.

Anger and bitterness welled inside her. How dare he move on to another woman when he'd left her empty and hollow inside?

When their son was gone?

She forced even, deep breaths in and out to steady the racing of her heart. She hadn't slept since Jordan had gone missing two days ago.

Damn Darren for not caring about his own son.

Letting her fury drive her, she whipped open

her car door, clenched the gun inside the pocket of her black hooded sweatshirt and scanned the area to make sure no one was watching. Except for Darren's truck and the shiny BMW that must belong to his long-legged lover girl, the parking lot was empty.

Well, hell, except there was a black SUV parked at the corner by some bushes. She studied it for a second, nerves clawing at her.

Thankfully it was empty.

She glanced back at the apartment and saw Darren padding naked to the bathroom. Uncaring that anyone could see them through the window, the woman dressed slowly, drawing out her movements as if she was performing.

If that was the kind of woman Darren wanted, why had he connected with her? Why had he gone to the trouble to act like he cared instead of just leaving their relationship at a one-night stand?

The answer hit her swift and hard. Because he'd wanted access to the money in her charity.

Tia inched up the sidewalk, taking cover in the overgrown bushes as the woman sashayed back through the apartment. Seconds later, Darren's lover opened the door, wobbling on heels that made Tia dizzy as she hurried to her fancy car and slipped inside.

Adrenaline shot through Tia as the car sped from the parking lot.

The bastard was alone.

She couldn't survive one more sleepless night without knowing what had happened to her son. At night, she heard his cries, saw his tiny little face looking at her with trust.

Trust she didn't deserve.

The wind picked up, rattling trees and sending leaves raining down. A cat darted out from behind a cottonwood, startling her, but she bit back a yelp.

She inched her way up the sidewalk to Darren's apartment door. His was the end unit, shrouded in bushes.

She scanned the parking lot and surrounding

area again as she reached for the door. Satisfied no one was watching, she turned the doorknob.

Shocking that the sleazy girl had actually locked it.

She bit her lip, then pulled the lock-picking tool she'd bought at the pawnshop from her pocket and jimmied the door. It squeaked as she opened it, and she paused, listening for Darren's footsteps or his voice.

The sound of the shower running soothed her nerves slightly.

A quick glance at the living room confirmed that Darren still hadn't mastered the art of picking up or cleaning. Dirty dishes filled a sink and clothes littered the sofa. A red bra hung from the end of a chair. The woman who'd just left or another lover?

Not that she cared who he screwed.

She just wanted to know where her son was.

Gripping the gun with both hands, she crept toward the bedroom. The low light burning accentuated the unmade, rumpled bed.

Her legs were trembling, so she sank into the wing chair by the dresser facing the bathroom door, then laid the gun in her lap and wiped her sweaty palms on her jeans.

Seconds dragged into minutes. Tension coiled inside her. Anger made her stomach churn.

But a calmness swept over her as the water kicked off. Tonight she would get some answers.

The shower door slammed in the bathroom. Footsteps sounded. Darren was humming.

A nervous giggle bubbled in her throat.

Darren stepped from the bathroom, wrapping a towel around his waist. His chest and hair were damp, and he was smiling.

When he spotted her, his smile faded.

She lifted the gun and aimed it at his chest. He was going to tell her the truth or she'd kill him.

RYDER LIFTED HIS binoculars and focused on Darren Hoyt's apartment, his instincts on full alert as Tia Jeffries confronted the man.

When Ryder first arrived at Tia's house, she'd

been running to her car like she was on a mission. Then she'd tucked that gun inside her purse and his instincts had kicked in.

Dread had knotted his stomach as he'd followed her to Hoyt's apartment. For a while, she'd sat perusing the parking lot, and he'd thought she might abandon whatever plan she had tonight.

No such luck.

She'd watched Darren screw some woman, waiting patiently as if the scene didn't disturb her.

Then she'd slid from the car and slunk up to the apartment.

A movement inside Hoyt's apartment snagged his eye.

The lights flickered in the bedroom. Movement as Darren, wearing nothing but a towel, stalked toward Tia.

Maybe they'd gotten rid of the baby together and this was rendezvous time.

A shadow moved. Tia standing now.

The silhouette of her body revealed an outstretched hand.

No, not outstretched. An arm extended, hand closed around a gun.

He jerked the door to his SUV open and ran toward the apartment.

Just as he reached the apartment, a gunshot rang out.

Chapter Two

Tia's hand trembled as she fired a shot at Darren's feet. "Tell me what you did with Jordan."

Darren jumped back, his eyes blazing with fear and shock. "What the hell are you doing, Tia?"

She lifted the gun and aimed it at his chest. "I want the truth, Darren. Where is my baby?"

"I told you I don't know." He took a step backward. "Now put down that damn gun. You don't want to hurt me."

Oh, but she did. "Maybe I do," she said, allowing her anger at his betrayal to harden her voice. "You cheated on me, emptied my bank account, then left me pregnant and alone." Thank God she'd had the good sense to protect her charity so he couldn't touch those funds.

The eyes that Tia had once thought were alluring darkened to a menacing scowl. "I wouldn't have cheated if you'd satisfied me, baby."

Oh, my God. He was a total jerk. "I don't care who you sleep with or how many women you have. All I want is my son."

His eyes narrowed. "You're the one who lost him," Darren said sharply. "So tell me what *you* did with him, Tia?"

Rage boiled inside Tia. "I was exhausted from labor and the night feedings. I went to sleep." Still, the guilt clawed at her. "That's when you snuck in and stole him, didn't you? You were mad that I wouldn't give you more money, so you decided to get revenge. Did you hurt him or leave him with someone?"

"You're crazy," Darren shouted. "I can't believe the cops haven't already locked you up."

She was terrified they would. Then she couldn't find her baby.

He reached for his cell phone on the bed. "I'm calling them now—"

Panicked, she fired the gun again. The bullet zinged by his hand. He pulled it back and cursed. She started toward him, but a low voice from behind her made her pause.

"Put down the weapon, Tia."

A chill swept through her at the gruff male voice. She clenched the gun with a white-knuckled grip and pivoted slightly to see who'd entered the room.

"Put it down, Tia," a big, broad-shouldered man with dark brown hair said. "No one needs to get hurt here."

"She's insane. She tried to kill me," Darren screeched.

Tia inhaled a deep breath at the sight of the man's Glock aimed at her.

"He stole my baby," Tia cried. "I just want him to tell me where Jordan is." She swung the gun back toward Darren. She'd come too far to stop now. If this man worked for Darren, she didn't intend to turn over her weapon. Then she'd never convince Darren to talk.

Suddenly the big man lunged toward her. She screamed as he knocked her arm upward, twisted the other one behind her back and growled in her ear, "I said drop it."

"Who are you?" Tia said on a moan. It felt as if he was tearing her arm out of the socket.

"Special Agent Ryder Banks. FBI."

Shock robbed her of breath. Or maybe it was his strong hold.

A second later, he whipped the Saturday night special from her hand. She cried out as he pushed her up against the wall, and yanked her other arm behind her.

The sound of metal clicking together sent despair through her as he handcuffed her and guided her to a chair.

"You saw her. She tried to kill me," Darren shouted.

Tears blurred Tia's eyes. If she went to jail, she'd never find her son.

RYDER NEVER LIKED being rough with a woman. But he had no choice. This one was about to shoot a man.

Whether the guy deserved it, he didn't know. He wished to hell he'd had more time to do a background check on both of these two.

"Thanks, man." Darren released an exaggerated breath and gestured toward Tia. "She's a total nut job. She was going to kill me."

"I was not." Tia shot him a rage-filled look. "I just want to know what you did with our baby."

"You fired at me," Darren shouted.

Ryder jerked a thumb toward Darren. "Sit down and shut up."

Darren sputtered an oath. "I didn't do anything. She broke in and pulled a gun on me."

Unfortunately she had done that—Ryder had witnessed it himself.

Perspiration beaded on Darren's forehead. "Arrest her and take her to jail."

Tia started to argue, but Ryder threw up a

warning hand, then addressed Darren. "Do you know where the baby is?"

A vein throbbed in the man's neck. "No." He tightened the towel around his waist.

"Put on some damn clothes," Ryder said, annoyed that the man hadn't asked to get dressed.

Darren sauntered to the closet, yanked out a shirt and jeans, then disappeared into the bathroom.

Tia cleared her throat. "I wasn't going to kill him," she said again. "I just wanted to scare him into talking."

Ryder's gaze met hers. His boss had failed to mention that Tia Jeffries was gorgeous. Petite in height, but curvy with big, bright blue eyes that made her look innocent and sexy at the same time.

An intoxicating combination.

"You should have let the police handle it," he said, forcing a hardness into his statement. He had to do his job, find the truth, ignore the fact that when he'd handcuffed her, he'd felt a shiver ripple through her. That she felt fragile—well, except for that gun.

Still, she wasn't experienced with it. Her hand had been shaking so badly he'd had to wrestle the gun from her before she hurt her ex or shot herself.

"I tried," she said, anger mingling with desperation in her voice. "But that sheriff treated me like I'd hurt my own baby. He believed Darren instead."

"That's because Tia is unstable," Darren said as he stepped into the bedroom. "She did something to Jordan and now she's trying to blame me."

"That's not true." Tia's voice broke. "I would never hurt my son. I…love him."

She said *love* in the present tense. A sign that she might be telling the truth. Sometimes when people were questioned about the suspicious disappearance of a loved one, they used past tense, which meant they already knew their loved one was dead.

"She has emotional problems," Darren said. "Just check her history. She had a breakdown a few years ago."

Ryder raised a brow. "Yet you married her?"

The man's eye twitched. "Hell, I didn't know it at the time. But then she started acting weird and depressed and erratic. I encouraged her to get help, but she refused."

Hurt flickered in Tia's eyes. "That's not true."

"Yes, it is. When we met, she was all over me. Later, I realized that was just because she wanted a baby." His voice grew bolder. "I guess she thought she could trap me into staying with her. And I fell for it. But she was obsessed with the pregnancy. She stockpiled baby clothes and toys and furniture for months."

Tia's eyes glistened with tears. "It's true I wanted a baby, but I wasn't obsessed."

Ryder folded his arms. Some women did that to trap a man. Then again, if Darren hadn't wanted a child, he had motive to do something to the infant.

"You must have been angry when you discovered you were going to be a father," he said, scrutinizing Darren for a reaction.

"He was," Tia said. "But I didn't get pregnant on purpose."

"Yes, she did." Darren's eyes flickered with anger. "And, yeah, sure, I was mad, but I took responsibility."

The bastard made it sound as if he'd done Tia a favor, not as if he actually cared about his own offspring.

Darren pasted on a smile that looked as phony as a three-dollar bill. "I stayed with her for a couple of months, but she's impossible to live with." Another exaggerated sigh, as if he was a victim of a crazy woman. "She pushed me away, told me she wanted me gone. That she'd just used me to get the child and she didn't need me anymore."

Pain streaked Tia's face as she shook her head in denial. "That's not the way it happened at all. He started cheating on me, dipping into my money."

Ryder studied Darren then Tia. No wonder the local sheriff had asked for help.

Both stories were plausible.

Although Darren's attitude rubbed him the wrong way. The man seemed too slick, as if lying came easy.

The anguish in Tia's eyes seemed real.

Although her anguish could stem from guilt.

He steeled himself against the tears in her deep blue eyes.

He would find out the truth.

No child should have to suffer at the hands of the very people who were supposed to love and protect him.

THE COLD METAL felt heavy on Tia's wrists.

She could go to prison for attempted murder.

God…where had this federal agent come from? Had he been following her?

And why? Because the local sheriff had passed

her case to the feds and thought she was guilty of doing something to Jordan?

Pain made her stomach clench. How could anyone think that?

She gulped back a sob. What was going to happen now?

She had to convince Agent Banks that she was telling the truth.

Darren strode across the room as if he owned the world and grabbed his belt. "Are you going to take her in?"

"You intend to press charges?" the agent asked.

Darren paused, his mouth forming a scowl. "I should. She would have killed me if you hadn't shown up."

"Don't do this, Darren. You know I'm not crazy or violent." Her voice cracked. "I just want my little boy back."

The agent crossed his arms. Darren walked over and stared into Tia's eyes with a coldness that chilled Tia to the bone. "Then tell the cops what you did with him and maybe they'll find him. And stop trying to make me sound like the guilty one."

Tia jutted up her chin, battling a sob. Her arms were beginning to ache from being bound behind her. "He's your son, Darren. But you really don't care about him, do you? If you did, you'd be asking the police to search for him, too."

"How do I even know he's mine?" Darren asked sarcastically. "Maybe you lied so I'd hang around."

Hurt robbed her of speech. How could he be so cruel?

Giving her one last icy look, he turned to the agent. "Lock her up so I don't have to worry about her shooting me tonight in my sleep."

"Darren, please," Tia whispered, desperate. "If you know who took Jordan, tell me. I won't even press charges. I just want him back."

Instead of answering, his jaw hardened. "Agent Banks, I told you to get her out of here. I have things to do."

A hopeless feeling engulfed Tia as the agent helped her stand.

"You need to come to the sheriff's office to file an official police report," the agent told Darren.

Darren gave a quick nod and muttered that he would.

Tia searched the agent's face for some hope that he believed her story, that he would help her.

But hope faded as he guided her outside to his car.

Dark storm clouds rolled in, obliterating the few stars that had shined earlier.

He opened the back door and gestured for her to get in. Emotions overwhelmed her as she sank into the backseat and he drove toward the jail.

Chapter Three

Tia hunched in the backseat of the agent's car, her nerves raw.

She was going to jail. She'd never see her baby again. If Darren had given Jordan to someone else, little Jordan would grow up without ever knowing her.

He might never know she'd looked for him, that she loved him.

A hollow emptiness welled in her chest. Hands still cuffed behind her, she leaned forward. She couldn't breathe.

Tears trickled down her cheeks, but she was helpless to wipe them away.

She closed her eyes, willing herself to be

strong. An image of her son's tiny body nestled in the baby blue blanket and cap she'd knitted taunted her.

Even if she never got him back, she had to know he was safe.

But how could she do that locked in a cell?

The car bounced over a rut in the road, and she lifted her head and looked out the window. Rugged farm and ranch land passed by. Trees swayed in the wind, leaves raining down. Dark shadows hovered along the deserted stretch of land, signaling that night had set in.

Another night away from her baby boy.

Minutes crawled by, turning into half an hour.

She gulped back a sob and cleared her throat. "Where are you taking me?"

Agent Banks met her gaze in the rearview mirror. "The sheriff's office in Sagebrush."

Despair threatened again. The sheriff, Dan Gaines, had been less than sympathetic when she'd asked for help. He'd practically accused her of killing her child so she could be single, footloose and fancy-free.

He had no idea that footloose and fancy-free was the last thing she wanted.

Or that she'd spent her adult life missing the family she'd lost. That all she wanted was someone to love to fill the hole in her aching heart.

That she spent her days working with kids and families in need, helping them find housing and counseling so they could patch their lives back together. That the money she'd received from her parents' life insurance had gone toward a charity she'd started called Crossroads.

Agent Banks drove through the small, quaint town of Sagebrush, then parked at the sheriff's office. Dread made her stomach roil.

She had to find someone who'd believe her. Sheriff Gaines certainly hadn't.

Maybe Agent Banks would.

Somehow she had to convince him she wasn't the lunatic Darren had painted her to be.

RYDER CLENCHED THE steering wheel with a white-knuckled grip. Tia Jeffries looked tiny and frightened, and so damn vulnerable that he felt like a jerk for handcuffing her.

She had a damn gun and shot at a man.

Whether she'd been provoked made no difference. The law was the law. He was a by-the-book man.

Except sometimes there were grays…

Where did this woman fall on the spectrum?

He parked at the sheriff's office, killed the engine, then walked to the back of the car and opened the door. Tia looked up at him with the saddest expression he'd ever seen.

Eyes that could suck a man in with that sparkling color and innocence.

Except the innocence was yet to be proven.

He had to keep his head clear, his emotions out of the picture.

Only her lower lip quivered as he took her arm and helped her from the vehicle, making his gut tighten.

"I don't care what you do to me," she said with a stubborn lift to her chin. "But please find my baby."

What could he say to that? She wasn't pleading for him to release her, but she was worried about her child.

Wasn't the sheriff looking for the baby?

His gaze met hers. "I'll find him," he said. And if she was lying, he'd make sure she stayed locked up.

But…if there was any truth to her story, he'd find that out, too.

She inhaled sharply as he led her to the door of the sheriff's office. When they entered, a husky man in a deputy's uniform sat at the desk. He looked up with a raised brow.

"Where's the sheriff?" Ryder asked.

"On a call." The man stood and extended his hand. "Deputy Hawthorne." He gave Tia a once-over. "What's going on?"

"Miss Jeffries needs to cool down awhile.

Pulled a gun on her ex." He didn't add that she'd fired that weapon.

The deputy grabbed a set of keys, jiggling them in his hand. "I'll put her in a holding cell."

Ryder nodded, although the terrified look on Tia's face twisted his insides. Dammit, he didn't have a choice.

"Can I have my phone call?" Tia asked.

"In time," Deputy Hawthorne said.

"Let her make the call," Ryder said. For some reason, he didn't trust how quickly the deputy planned to follow through.

Deputy Hawthorne shrugged and gestured toward the phone. "Is it local?"

Tia nodded, and he handed her the handset. The handcuffs jangled as she punched in a number.

Ryder gestured for the deputy to step to the side. "Miss Jeffries claims her baby was kidnapped from her home. Has the sheriff been investigating?"

The man shrugged. "He thinks she got rid of the kid. No proof yet, though."

"Anything on the Amber Alert?"

"So far nothing."

"He talked to the baby's father, Darren Hoyt?"

Deputy Hawthorne nodded. "Man had an alibi."

Ryder wondered how solid it was. "Did the sheriff tape his interview with Miss Jeffries?"

The deputy narrowed his eyes. "Not when he got the call and went to her house. But she came in and he recorded that conversation."

"I'd like to watch the tape."

Hawthorne worked his mouth side to side. "Maybe you should wait on the sheriff to return."

"I can look at it here or get a warrant and take the tape with me, so why not make it easy on both of us?"

The deputy seemed to think it over, then muttered agreement. Tia hung up the phone, her hands trembling as she placed them back on her lap. Hawthorne wasted no time. He escorted her through the back to a holding cell. Ryder scanned the space as he followed. Two cells. The other was empty.

At least she wasn't being thrown in with some dangerous derelict. He removed the handcuffs before he motioned her inside.

The cell door closed with a clang. Tia looked small and helpless behind those bars, yet he'd seen the fight in her when she'd confronted her ex.

"Please find Jordie," she whispered in a pained voice. "He's just a few weeks old. He…needs me."

Yes, he did.

But Ryder had seen the worst of society on that last case. The head of the damn ring had seemed like an upstanding citizen. But evil had lurked beneath the surface.

Did Tia deserve to have her son back?

For the life of him, he wanted to believe her.

Maybe because no kid should grow up thinking his mother had gotten rid of him like Ryder had.

"I will find the baby." And he'd put away whoever had taken the child.

He gestured to the deputy. "The video?"

The man frowned but led him to a small office across the hall from the cells. Another room was designated for interrogations.

Ryder took a seat. Seconds later, Hawthorne started the video feed of his initial interview at his office with Tia after her son disappeared.

Ryder knotted his hands in his lap as he watched the recording.

Tia paced the interrogation room. "Sheriff, you have to find my baby. I think my ex did something to him." She looked haggard in a worn T-shirt and jeans, her hair yanked back in a ponytail and her eyes swollen from crying.

Sheriff Gaines, a robust man with a scar above his left eye, pointed to a chair. "Sit down. Then tell me what happened again."

"I don't want to sit down," Tia cried. "I want you to find Jordan."

Sheriff Gaines jerked a thumb toward the chair, his voice brusque. "I said sit down."

Tia heaved a breath and sank into the chair in front of the rickety wooden table. She fidgeted with a tissue, wiping her eyes then shredding it into pieces. "I think Darren is responsible."

Sheriff Gaines folded his beefy arms on the table. "Start at the beginning and tell me what happened."

"For God's sake, we went through this when I first called you yesterday." Tia ran a hand through the front of her tangled hair. "Jordie is only six weeks old." She pressed a hand over her chest. "I fed him at midnight the night before, and he fell asleep in my arms." A smile curved her mouth as if she was remembering. "He's so little, and he eats every three hours, so I was exhausted from being up at night." She looked down at her hands. "I shouldn't have, but I laid him in the crib, then went to my room and crawled on my bed. I was only going to close my eyes for a minute, but I must have fallen into a deep sleep."

Instead of reassuring her that it was okay to rest while her baby slept, the sheriff grunted. "Go on."

Guilt streaked her face. "Anyway, a little while later, a noise woke me up."

"A noise?" the sheriff asked. "The baby crying?"

"No." Tia closed her eyes and rubbed her temple as if she was trying to remember. When she opened her eyes again, she exhaled a shaky breath. "It sounded like a gunshot, but then I realized it was a car. Backfiring. I looked out the window and saw taillights racing away." She rubbed her arms now as she paced. "Then I went to check on Jordan, but…his crib was empty."

A heartbeat passed, the silence thick with tension. "You believe that someone broke into your house and stole your baby while you were asleep?"

Tia nodded miserably. “I told you that already. I usually put him in the cradle by my bed, but I’d been rocking him in the nursery so I left him alone in there. I…thought I’d hear him if he woke up.”

The fact that she’d varied her routine must have struck the sheriff as suspicious, because a scowl darkened his face. “So the one night you put him in the other room, he disappears?”

Tia nodded. “It’s all my fault. I should have put him in the cradle, but I’d barely slept since he was born and I wasn’t thinking.”

“I see. You were exhausted and tired of dealing with a fussy baby, so you left the baby where you couldn’t hear him,” Sheriff Gaines said.

“No.” Tia stopped pacing long enough to throw up her hands. “That’s not what I meant! But I thought he’d be safe in his nursery and I was only going to take a nap, and we were alone.” Her voice cracked and she dropped into the chair again. “But someone came in and stole him.”

The sheriff leaned forward, arms still folded.

"Don't you mean that you were sick of taking care of a crying infant so you wanted to get rid of him? Maybe you lost it and smothered him, then you panicked and buried him in the yard or put him in the trash."

"No, God, no!" Horror turned Tia's skin a pale color. "That's not what happened. I love my baby—"

"It happens, Miss Jeffries. Mothers are exhausted, suffering from postpartum depression. They can't take it anymore and they snap. They shake the baby to get it to be quiet or they put it in the bed a little too hard or—"

"No!" Tia shouted. "I love my son. I came here for your help, not for you to accuse me of hurting my son." She launched herself at the man and grabbed his shirt. "You have to do something. Look for him!"

The sheriff gripped her hands and pried them from his shirt. "Listen, Miss Jeffries, it'll be easier on you if you cooperate. Tell me what you did with your baby. Maybe he's still alive and we can save him."

Tia sucked in a sharp breath. "I didn't do anything with him except feed him and put him to bed. I think my ex took him."

"Why would he do that?" Gaines asked.

"Because he didn't want a baby in the first place."

"But you got pregnant anyway," the sheriff said in a voice laced with accusations. "You thought if you got pregnant he wouldn't leave you, didn't you?" Sheriff Gaines growled. "Then you had the baby and he left anyway, so you did something to the kid and are trying to get revenge by blaming him."

Tia shook her head vehemently. "No," she cried. "Please believe me."

The sheriff set her away from him. "I will investigate, Miss Jeffries. In fact, my deputy and I are going to search your place again now."

Ryder chewed the inside of his cheek. Gaines

was playing tough cop, pushing Tia, just as he might have done.

But had he ignored the possibility that Tia might be telling the truth?

Had he even checked into Tia's ex or canvassed the neighbors to see if anyone had heard that car backfire or seen someone snooping around Tia's place?

Ryder's phone buzzed. He checked the number.

McCullen.

Dammit. He hadn't planned on ever talking to the family.

But one of them had obviously found him.

What the hell was he going to do about it?

Chapter Four

Ryder checked the video where the sheriff interviewed Darren.

Hoyt seemed cocky, self-assured. He insisted he hadn't been in Tia's house and that he hadn't taken the baby. He also accused Tia of trying to trap him into marriage, just as he'd told Ryder.

Had the bastard practiced his story?

For some reason, the sheriff didn't push Hoyt. Didn't pursue his past or the financial angle.

Because he'd decided that Tia was the guilty party.

"Hell, Tia was jealous that I was moving on with my life," Darren said. "She probably faked the kidnapping to get my attention, hoping I'd come back to her."

Damn. The federal agent in him agreed that Darren's story was plausible.

But Tia didn't appear to be in love with Darren—she was only concerned about the baby.

Although it was true that the parents were always suspects in a child's kidnapping, disappearance or death. He couldn't clear her just yet.

But what if she was telling the truth?

Just because his parents had sold him didn't mean this woman had done the same thing. But if she had, he'd make sure she paid.

He didn't give a damn if her hair looked like sunshine and her blue eyes poured tears as big as a waterfall.

Or if she looked terrified and pale. That could be explained from guilt. Criminals or people who committed crimes in a fit of passion often experienced guilt.

Sometimes they imploded on themselves.

Unless they were pathological liars or sociopaths.

But she didn't fit that profile.

He had to run background checks on both of them, look at their computers, phone records, talk to neighbors and friends.

He scrubbed a hand over his bleary eyes, a good night's sleep beckoning. But the image of Tia in that cell made him decide to put bed on hold for a while, at least until he did some work.

He shut off the tapes, phoned his boss and requested warrants, then stepped back into the front office. The deputy was leaning back in his desk chair, feet propped on the desk, a grin on his face.

"Yeah, Martha, I should be there in about an hour."

Ryder folded his arms and stared at the man, sending him the silent message to get off the phone.

The deputy scowled, tilted his head sideways

so Ryder couldn't hear his conversation, then ended the call.

The idea of Tia sitting alone in a dark cell all night rubbed Ryder the wrong way. "You're leaving the woman alone in here tonight?"

Hawthorne frowned. "The night shift deputy is coming in. Why? That woman probably killed her kid. She deserves to rot in prison."

Anger shot through Ryder. "Have you ever heard the phrase *innocent until proven guilty*?"

Hawthorne barked a laugh. "Yeah, but don't let those blue eyes fool you."

"What makes you so sure she's the culprit? Why not the baby's father? He didn't want a child in the first place."

Hawthorne cut his gaze to the side. "I know women, that's why."

Ryder leaned forward, hands on the desk, body coiled with tension. "Just make sure she's safe in there," he said in a low growl.

A muscle ticked in the deputy's jaw. "I know how to do my job."

Ryder gritted his teeth. Small-town sheriffs and deputies disliked the feds encroaching on their territory.

"Did you need something else?" Hawthorne asked.

Ryder met his gaze with a stony look. "Darren Hoyt is supposed to come in and file an official report. Let me know if he shows up."

Hawthorne gave a clipped nod.

"Do you have Miss Jeffries and Hoyt's computers?"

"The sheriff already looked at them but didn't find anything."

"Phone records?"

Hawthorne shrugged. "Have to ask Sheriff Gaines."

"I will." But he'd prefer to look at them himself anyway, especially since the deputy and sheriff had already made their decision about Tia's guilt.

Ryder tossed his business card on the desk.

"Let me know if you hear anything." He didn't wait for a response.

Even if the sheriff had investigated thoroughly, which it didn't appear he had, Ryder would conduct his own inquiry.

If Jordan had been kidnapped for money, Tia would have received a ransom call.

Which meant whoever took him had a different motive.

Worse—every day this baby was missing meant the chance of finding him diminished.

TIA SHIVERED AS she hunched on the only piece of furniture in the cell—a tiny cot. The low lights in the small hallway barely lit the inside of the tiny barred room. A threadbare blanket lay on top of a single mattress that was so thin you could feel the metal springs beneath it.

Tia curled her arms around her waist, clenching her fingers into her palms so tightly she felt the pain of her fingernails stabbing her skin.

She deserved the pain. She was a terrible

mother. If she hadn't fallen asleep, her baby wouldn't have been taken.

How could she have been so deep in sleep that she hadn't heard someone break into the house?

The sheriff said there were no signs of a break-in.

But there had to be.

Unless she'd been so exhausted she'd forgotten to lock the door.

No...she always locked the door. She was compulsive about it and checked it at least three times a night.

A squeaking noise alerted her to the fact that someone had opened the door between the cells and the front office. Footsteps echoed on the concrete floor.

Her stomach knotted. Had Sheriff Gaines returned to make more accusations? To taunt her?

A big, hulking shadow moved across the dimly lit hall. More footsteps. A breath rattled in the quiet.

She tightened her hands again in an attempt

to hold herself together and braced herself for whatever Gaines or his deputy dished out.

"Tia?"

She jerked her head up. Not Gaines's snide voice. Special Agent Ryder Banks.

God, had he come back to rescue her from this nightmare?

He stopped in front of the cell, his big body taking up so much air that she could barely breathe. Then he shoved a notepad and pen through the bars. "I need you to write down all your contacts. The people you work with, your friends, neighbors, anyone you can think of who might vouch for you or who had access to your house."

Hope warred with despair. What if it was too late?

"Tia?" This time his voice was gruff. Commanding. "If you want my help, take the pad and start writing."

She pulled herself from her stupor, stood on shaking legs and crossed the small space. Her hand trembled as she grabbed the pad and pen. "You're going to help me?"

Silence stretched for a full minute while he stared at her. She felt his scrutiny as if he was dissecting her.

"I'll find your son. Then I'll make whoever kidnapped him pay."

The coldness in his tone suggested he hadn't decided on her innocence yet.

But at least he was going to investigate. That was a lot more than Gaines had done.

She sighed, then walked back to the cot, sank onto the mattress and began the list.

Her coworkers and the volunteers at the shelter came first. Two of her neighbors next.

"Don't leave anyone out," he said.

She ignored the distrust in his tone. As long as he looked for her son, she could put up with anything. "I won't. Are you going to have Darren do this, too?"

"Absolutely." He paused, then cleared his

throat. "You said you run a charity for families in need. Is this for abused women and children?"

Tia shrugged. "Yes. But it's also open to anyone who needs help. Sometimes mothers come to us when their husbands or children's fathers abandon them. They need help finding housing and food and jobs. We've also had families in crisis—it could be drug or alcohol related, one of them has lost his job, even a long-term illness where the parent has to go into a hospital for treatment. We work through social services, but we also find temporary foster homes through local churches and provide counseling to help them get back on their feet. Our goal is to keep the family intact or to reunite them if there's a separation period."

"Admirable." His dark eyes narrowed. "Can you think of anyone you've angered? Maybe a father or mother who lost their kids to the system, someone who'd want revenge against you."

Tia's pulse jumped. There were a couple of names.

"Write them down," he said as if he'd read her mind.

Tia nodded, then scribbled every name she could think of, including the hospital staff and attendants as well as Amy, a young delivery nurse, who'd befriended her.

Finally she handed the agent the list. Her fingers brushed his big hands, and a tingle of something dangerously like attraction shot through her.

She yanked her hand back quickly. She'd never be foolish enough to fall for another man.

When she got Jordan back, he would be the only one in her life.

RYDER LEFT TIA, shaken by the spark of electricity he'd felt when she'd touched his hand. Then she'd looked up at him with those damn sea-like blue eyes and he'd thought he would drown in them.

She had some kind of pull on him.

A pull he had to ignore.

He was a loner. Always had been. Always would be. There was no place for a woman or family in his line of work.

It was still odd, since he wasn't usually drawn to gun-carrying women who shot at their husbands or to suspects in his cases.

His reaction had to be due to lack of sleep. He wasn't thinking clearly.

He needed that beer and a bed. Although an image of Tia sprawled naked on the sheets with her hair fanned out taunted him.

He shook the image away.

The list of names in his hand meant he had work to do. Sleep would have to wait.

He just prayed Tia would be safe in that cell. At least she couldn't get herself in any more trouble by killing her ex.

He bypassed Hawthorne, who was on the telephone again, strode outside to his SUV and headed toward Crossroads. Although it was getting late in the evening, hopefully someone would still be awake.

The old Victorian house was nestled on an acre of land literally at the crossroads of the town limits and the countryside. The porch light and lights inside were on, indicating someone was there.

Ryder swung down the drive, surprised at the wildflowers growing in patches along the drive. A cheery-looking sign in blue and white boasted its name, and underneath, etchings of children and parents linking hands in a circle as if united had been carved into the wood.

He passed a barn and spotted two horses galloping on a hill to the east.

Rocking chairs and porch swings filled the wraparound porch, making the place look homey and inviting.

He climbed the porch, wiped his feet on the welcome mat, and banged the door knocker, which was shaped like the sun. Through the window, he noted a kitchen with a large round oak table and a woman at the sink washing dishes.

A second later, a twentysomething blonde with pale green eyes opened the door. She couldn't be more than five feet tall and couldn't weigh a hundred pounds. Her eyes widened as her gaze traveled from his face down to his size-thirteen boots and back to his face.

He flashed his identification. "Special Agent Ryder Banks, FBI. I need to ask you some questions about Tia Jeffries."

She blinked, a wariness in her expression. "Yes, Tia told me you'd probably be coming. I'm Elle Grist, Tia's assistant."

"When did she tell you I was coming?"

"When she called after you arrested her," the woman said, disapproval lacing her tone.

So she'd used her one phone call to call the charity. Why? To request they cover for her?

"Before you even ask, no, Tia would never do anything to hurt her baby or anyone else. She's the most loving, caring person on this planet."

"You're loyal to her. I get that."

"Yes, I am, but with good reason," Elle said.

"Tia lost her family—every one of them—on the day of her college graduation. They were flying to the ceremony when the plane went down." Her voice cracked with emotion. "She still blames herself. More than anything in the world, she values family. That's why she started this place. She's helped so many people over the past five years that she deserves a medal."

Elle dabbed at her eyes. "Tia also took me in when I lost my mother two years ago. She let me live with her until I could get a job. She saved me from…"

Ryder arched a brow. "From what?"

Elle rubbed a finger over a scar on her wrist. "I wouldn't be alive if it weren't for her." Footsteps sounded, and the heavyset woman he'd seen through the window washing dishes appeared, drying her hands on a checked cloth.

"Miss Elle speaks the gospel. Everyone loves Miss Tia." She planted her beefy hands on her hips. "You gonna find the evil one that took her baby?"

Ryder swallowed, choosing his words carefully. From Tia's list, he guessed this woman must be Ina, the cook and housekeeper. "I'm certainly going to try. But I need your help."

"We'll do anything for Tia," Ina said.

He gestured to the notepad. "Then let me come in. I want you to look over this list Tia made and tell me about the people on it."

The women exchanged questioning looks, then a silent agreement passed between them, and they motioned for him to enter.

"Just be quiet now," Ina said. "We have two families here with little ones. Took their mamas forever to get them to sleep tonight."

Ryder glanced at the stairs and nodded. It certainly appeared that Tia was some kind of saint to these people. If that was the case, who had stolen her son?

And what had they done with the little boy?

Chapter Five

Ryder studied the photos on the wall of Tia's office. She and the staff had taken pictures of several families who'd come through Crossroads and displayed them on the wall to showcase that their efforts were working.

Personalized thank-you notes and cards were interspersed, creating a collage that triggered Ryder's admiration.

"Darren Hoyt claims Tia is unstable, that she suffered from depression," Ryder said.

Elle's mouth grew pinched. "She is not unstable and she certainly doesn't suffer from depression."

"That girl had it rough a while back," Ina interjected. "Losing her mama and daddy and brother all at once. Anyone would have been grief stricken. On top of that, she blamed herself 'cause they were on their way to see her."

That would have been tough.

"She was only twenty-one at the time," Elle said. "She was suddenly alone and didn't know what to do. But one of her friends convinced her to go to an in-house therapy program. So she did. No shame in that."

No, he supposed not.

"I admire her," Elle continued. "She took her own personal tragedy and used it to make her stronger and to help others by building this place."

That was admirable. Ryder addressed Ina. "What did you think about Darren Hoyt?"

Ina folded her arms. "He was a con man. He knew Tia had money from her folks and married her to get hold of it. But that girl was smart and set up the charity so no one could touch it."

A wise move. "She didn't trust Darren from the beginning?" Ryder asked.

Elle shrugged. "It wasn't that. She just wanted to protect her family's money and for their deaths to stand for something."

"She barely paid herself a salary," Ina said. "But she gave openly to others."

"When Darren realized he would never get her inheritance, he left her," Elle said. "That man was a manipulative SOB—he never loved her."

"She loved him?" Ryder asked, wondering why that thought bothered him.

Elle blew out a breath. "At first I think she did."

"She was young, vulnerable, lonely and naive," Ina said. "Darren Hoyt took advantage of that."

Ryder gritted his teeth. "Do you think she was jealous that he moved on? She wouldn't have done something to get Darren's attention and win him back?"

"Heavens, no," Ina murmured.

Elle shook her head. "Tia had never seemed happier than during that pregnancy."

Ina smiled softly. "She wanted that baby more than anything."

Ryder rubbed his chin. "Can you think of anyone who'd want to hurt her? Maybe someone whose family came through Crossroads?"

Both women shook their heads no.

He consulted the notepad. "Tell me about Bennett Jones."

"He was furious when his wife left him and took their son," Ina said.

"Do you think he kidnapped Tia's little boy for revenge?" Elle asked.

Ryder shifted on the balls of his feet. "I don't know—do *you* think he did?"

Elle chewed her bottom lip. "It's hard to say how far he'd go. Tia suggested he attend anger-management classes."

"He did have a mean streak," Ina agreed, her cheeks puffing out.

Ryder checked the list again. “What about Wanda Hanson?”

Ina fanned herself. “Lord help, that woman had her issues.”

“What do you mean?” Ryder asked.

“She had back problems and became addicted to pain meds, then escalated to harder stuff,” Elle said. “Husband found her passed out while their baby was left unattended. They lived on a lake, and their toddler was outside alone.”

Ina tsked and shook her head. “It’s a wonder the little fellow didn’t drown.”

Ryder arched a brow. “What happened?”

“Father tried everything to convince her to get help. He finally divorced her and moved with the boy to Texas to be close to his folks.”

Ryder thanked Elle and Ina, then extended his business card. “Please call me if you think of anything else that could be helpful.”

Ina caught his arm. “Agent Banks, you gonna help our Tia?”

Ryder cleared his throat. These women had

sung Tia's praises. If everything they said was true, she was a victim. "I'm going to find Jordan," he said.

Both women nodded, and he headed out the door.

If Bennett and Wanda had lost custody of their children, they might blame Tia.

It was a place to start.

TIA COUNTED THE scratches on the wall of the cell beside the cot. Foul language mingled with crude sketches and another area where someone had drawn lines counting the days.

She wondered if she should start her own calendar.

A cold chill washed over her at the thought. Knowing Sheriff Gaines, he'd keep her locked up until he finished making his case against her for hurting her baby and she went to trial. Now, he'd probably add attempted murder for threatening Darren.

The blasted man. If he'd done his job and

found her son, she wouldn't have been forced to take matters into her own hands.

She stretched her fingers, shocked at herself for firing that gun. She'd never believed she had it in her to hurt another human.

Not until she'd held her baby. The very second she'd looked into his little face, she'd known she'd do anything to protect him.

Yet she'd failed.

Tears blurred her vision. She blinked in an attempt to hold them back, but it was futile. The enormity of her loss struck her again and she walked over to the bars of the cell and curled her fingers around them.

She had no idea what time it was, but the windowless cell and the dim light made it feel like it was the middle of the night.

She wrapped her arms around her waist, and rocked herself back and forth. She felt empty inside and ached to hold her little boy again.

Where was he now? Was he safe?

He ate every few hours. Was he hungry?

Just the thought of feeding him made her breasts throb. They'd shared a tender bond when she'd nursed him.

The tears broke through as she realized she might never get to hold him again. No one would ever love him as much as she did.

She just prayed that whoever had kidnapped him takes care of him and keeps him safe until she finds him.

And she *would* find him, no matter how long it took or what she had to do.

RYDER'S STOMACH GROWLED. He hadn't eaten all day. And he'd never gotten any sleep.

He would take care of the food, though, while he did a little research on Darren Hoyt.

He parked at the Sagebrush Diner, a place that reminded him of an old Western saloon. The log cabin sported rails outside to tie up horses. Considering the closest stable was twenty miles away, he doubted it was used much, but it was a nice touch.

Several cars filled the parking lot, and a group of teens had parked in the back corner and were sitting on the hoods of their cars hanging out. The flicker of a lighter lit the air, and smoke curled upward. Cigarettes or weed—he didn't know which.

Not that he cared at the moment. He had more important things to do—like finding Jordie Jeffries.

Country music blared from an old-fashioned jukebox in one corner, chatter and laughter buzzed through the room, and burgers sizzled on a griddle in the kitchen area. He claimed a seat at a booth just as a twentysomething waitress approached.

She gave him a once-over, then a big smile. "Hey, tall, dark and handsome, what can I get you?"

He bit back a chuckle at her attempt to flirt. He wasn't interested and didn't take the bait. "Burger, chili and a beer." He set his laptop on the table. "You have Wi-Fi?"

She nodded. "Finally. Password is Sagebrush."

The name of the diner—original.

He thanked her, then booted up his machine, ending the conversation. He quickly connected to the internet, then the FBI's database and plugged in Darren Hoyt's name.

A preliminary background check revealed the man had been born in Houston to a preacher and his wife, who'd died when Darren was in college. Had he used that fact to bond with Tia?

His work history showed that he'd dabbled in real estate and had touted himself as an entrepreneur. He'd lived in Montana and Colorado and had been single until he'd married Tia.

A couple of speeding tickets, but no charges filed against him. No rap sheet.

The waitress returned with his beer and food and he muttered thanks. Hoyt was no saint. If Elle and Ina were correct and he was a con man, there had to be something in his history that was suspicious.

He sipped his beer, then dug into the food.

By the time he'd finished, he'd found a photo of Darren online from a charity fund-raiser Tia had organized the year before and plugged it into facial recognition software.

Seconds later, he had a hit. Only the man in the photograph wasn't Darren Hoyt. His name was Bill Koontz.

Bill Koontz was born in a small town in Texas. His mother was Renee Koontz, who had a record for solicitation and had served prison time for drug dealing when her son was fifteen. He'd been in and out of foster homes for a few months, then lived on the streets. At eighteen, he'd disappeared for a while.

Around twenty-five, he resurfaced in Montana, where he'd worked odd jobs, then had become a groomer at a country club stable.

Several women at the club had reported that he'd swindled them out of their savings. Eventually the guy had served three years in prison. When he was released, he moved to Wyoming, where he eased his way back into another country club and resorted to his old tricks.

At first, life must have been good. But then reports of him trying to con members out of their savings cropped up, and he was fired.

Two years later, Darren Hoyt had been born. The name was new, but Ryder would bet his life that the con game had continued.

Tia had simply been a mark.

The waitress appeared, the flirtatious smile joined by a gleaming in her eyes. "Another beer, sugar?"

"Just the check." Another beer and she might take it as a sign that he was interested.

Her smile dipped into a frown and she handed him the bill. He tossed some cash the table to cover it, then dug around another minute for more information on Hoyt. Nothing again on that name.

Curious, he ran a search on country clubs in the area and found one about five miles from Crossroads.

His pulse jumped. Maybe Tia had approached members to donate to her charity.

He found the number and left a message identifying himself and asking for a return call from the director.

Exhaustion knotted his muscles, and he finally stood and left the diner. The waitress waved to him as he left, but he ignored her. He didn't have time for women.

Not when a baby needed him.

A HALF HOUR LATER, Ryder pulled down the drive to his cabin. An image of Tia alone in that prison cell sleeping on that cot taunted him.

From what he'd learned, she didn't deserve to be in jail. While she was locked up, her son's kidnapper was getting farther and farther away.

He had to do something.

Tomorrow he'd confront Darren about his past. Then maybe he'd persuade the man to talk.

Woods backed up to his cabin, trees swaying

in the wind. He'd chosen the place because it was virtually deserted, a retreat after working undercover or dealing with criminals.

He tucked his laptop beneath his arm, then climbed from the SUV, scanning the area for trouble as he always did. Once a detective, always a detective.

Satisfied the area was clear, he let himself into the cabin. He flipped on the light switch, then headed straight toward the shower. Before he could undress, a knock sounded at the door.

Startled, he gripped his gun and eased into the living room. He'd made too many enemies on the job to trust anyone.

He inched to the side window in front, eased the curtain aside and checked the yard. A beat-up pickup truck sat in the drive.

Hmm.

Holding his gun to his side, he stepped over to the front door and opened it.

Shock stole his breath at the sight of the man standing on his porch.

A man who looked like him.

It had to be his twin brother, Cash Koker.

Chapter Six

Ryder blinked to clear his vision. It was almost eerie, seeing himself yet knowing the man in front of him wasn't him. Same dark brown eyes, wide jaw, broad shoulders.

Except Cash looked freshly shaven where Ryder was scruffy, with three-day-old beard stubble on his jaw and hair that needed a wash and a trim.

Cash shoved his hands in the pockets of his denim jacket. "Damn," Cash muttered. "They told me I had a twin, but I couldn't believe it."

Words tangled on Ryder's tongue. He swallowed to make his voice work. "You knew about me?"

Cash shook his head. “Not until recently.” His gaze traveled up and down Ryder as if he too couldn’t believe what he was seeing. “You knew about me?”

Ryder shook his head. “Not until I saw that news report where Sheriff McCullen was interviewed.”

“That’s Maddox.” Cash glanced inside the cabin. “Uh, can I come in?”

Ryder squared his shoulders. Was he ready for this conversation? Hell, no.

But he had questions and couldn’t turn this man away, not when he looked so much like him it was shocking. They *were* brothers, twins.

And none of this was Cash’s fault. Judging from Maddox’s statement, Cash had only recently learned about the McCullens, too.

“Sure.” He stepped aside and gestured for Cash to enter, then led him to the small den. “Sorry this place is a wreck. I haven’t been here for a while.”

Cash studied him, arms folded. "You're with the FBI, aren't you?"

"Yes." Ryder clenched his jaw. "How did you know that? And how did you find me?"

Cash shrugged. "My—our—brothers have been looking for you awhile. Ray's a private investigator and Maddox used his connections in the sheriff's department to expedite the search."

Ryder gritted his teeth. What did you say to a brother you didn't know you had? "Do you want a beer or something?"

A small grin tugged at Cash's mouth. "Yeah. Thanks."

Ryder grabbed two cold ones from the refrigerator just to have something to do. He knew how to handle hardened criminals, but he had no idea how to handle this situation.

When he turned back, Cash was watching him. "Sorry for just showing up here." He popped the top of the beer and took a sip. "But once Ray found you, I…had to see for myself."

Ryder gave a nod of understanding, then gestured toward the back deck. It offered a great view of the woods and was his favorite spot to think and unwind after a case.

He and Cash stepped outside, a breeze stirring the warm air. Ryder claimed the rocker and Cash settled on the porch swing. It creaked back and forth as he pushed it with his feet, the silence between them thick with questions and the revelation that they were identical twins but also strangers who knew nothing about each other.

He sipped his beer, stalling.

"So how did you grow up?" Cash finally asked.

Ryder heaved a wary breath. "I was adopted by a couple named Troy and Myra Banks. They told me I was adopted when I was little, but not about my birth family."

Cash's jaw tightened.

"You weren't adopted?"

Cash shook his head. "Nope, I was sickly. Bounced from foster home to foster home."

Guilt gnawed at Ryder. "That must have been rough."

"I survived," Cash said, although the gruffness of his voice hinted that it had been tough.

No wonder Cash had welcomed the McCullen brothers.

"So how did you find out about the McCullens?" Ryder asked.

A sardonic chuckle escaped Cash and he swallowed another sip of beer. "A few months ago I got arrested. Maddox and Brett and Ray showed up at my bail hearing. Took me home with them and paid for my defense."

Ryder narrowed his eyes. "Just like that? No strings attached?"

Cash frowned. "Well, Maddox made it clear that if I was guilty he wouldn't cover for me. But they investigated and helped me clear my name."

Ryder stared at the sliver of moon trying to peek through the trees.

"Your turn," Cash said. "How did you find out about the McCullens?"

Ryder silently cursed. "After my dad died, I

became curious and did some digging. Finally I asked my mom."

"You mean your adopted mother?"

"Same thing," Ryder said, his loyalty to the woman who'd raised him kicking in. "She told me what happened."

Cash narrowed his eyes. "She told you that you were kidnapped, that your real mother died trying to find you?"

Ryder locked his jaw and debated what to say. But he refused to lie. "Not exactly."

"Then what did she tell you?"

Ryder leaned forward, arms braced on his thighs as he studied Cash. "That the McCullens needed money to expand their ranch, so they made a deal with a lawyer and sold me."

A startled look passed across Cash's face. "What? Damn, that's not the way it happened."

"How do you know?" Ryder asked. "We were both babies at the time."

Cash scraped a hand over his face, drawing

Ryder's gaze to the long scar on his forehead. Ryder's gut pinched. How had he gotten that?

Cash settled his Stetson on his lap. "That's right, but once the McCullens found me, they explained everything. It's a long story. The doctor who delivered us made a mistake with another delivery, a mistake that cost another couple their child. That baby's father stole us from the hospital to replace the child he lost, and the doctor covered out of guilt. He told our parents that we were stillborn."

Shock rolled through Ryder. "That's the story the McCullens told you?" Ryder said, well aware his comment sounded like an accusation. "How do you know it's true?"

Cash sucked in a sharp breath. "Because Maddox investigated. That doctor remained friends with the McCullens, especially Joe, our father. He finally admitted what happened—that Mom was murdered because she didn't believe we'd died and because she was searching for us. Dunn, the man who'd taken us, killed her to cover up the truth."

Ryder's mind raced. "If that's true, why didn't the man who kidnapped us raise us?"

Cash grunted. "Apparently his wife figured out what he'd done and insisted he take us back to the McCullens. The man was afraid of being arrested, so he dropped us off at a church instead."

Ryder swallowed hard. But Myra and Troy Banks claimed they'd gotten him from an attorney and led him to believe the McCullens orchestrated the deal. They hadn't mentioned anything about a church.

Ryder stood and walked to the edge of the deck. A wild animal growled from the woods. He could almost see its predator eyes glowing in the dark.

"Last year, our father, Joe, realized what had happened. He started looking for us, too. Then he was murdered."

Ryder drained his beer. "Listen, Cash, it

sounds like you had a rough childhood. I'm sure it feels good to think the McCullens want you." He balled his hand into a fist and pressed it over his chest. "But I have a family—a mother, at least. And I don't want or need the McCullens in my life."

Emotions wrestled in Cash's eyes. He'd obviously thought Ryder would be thrilled to learn about his roots.

Ryder might—if he didn't already know the real story. Of course the McCullen brothers wouldn't admit that their parents had been greedy enough to trade two of their children for money.

Cash removed a manila envelope from the inside of his jacket. He laid it on the coffee table. "Inside are letters and cards our mother wrote to you. I have an envelope just like it."

Ryder raised a brow in question.

"She—our mother, Grace—wrote to us after we went missing. She bought cards for Christmases and birthdays. Read them and you'll see I'm telling the truth."

Without another word, Cash set his empty beer bottle on the table with a thud, then strode back through the house and outside. Ryder stared at the envelope, his heart pounding, until he heard Cash's truck spring to life and chug away.

Anger and resentment mingled with doubt. He squashed the doubt. His mother loved him. She wouldn't have lied to him.

He didn't need any letters or cards or for his life to be disrupted by the McCullens.

He was fine on his own. He always had been. He always would be.

THE HOURS DRAGGED BY. Tia had felt alone when her family had died, but she'd never felt more alone than she did now, without her baby in her arms.

Her eyes felt gritty from staring at the ceiling of the jail cell, and her body ached from fatigue.

But that discomfort was nothing compared to the emptiness inside her.

She might never see Jordie again.

She'd read stories about children who went missing and were never recovered. There were other accounts where the child was located years later but had bonded with whoever had raised them.

Jordie was only an infant. Babies changed every day. What if it took months or years to find him and she didn't even recognize him?

She paced the cell for the millionth time, mentally retracing the events of the past couple of days.

Darren had moved out months ago. But he'd contacted her two weeks before she was due, offering to set up a fund for the baby—with her money. He wanted to invest in a surefire project that would double the money in a week's time.

She had refused. At that point, she didn't trust him. He'd already cleaned out her savings account and most of her checking account.

He could have kidnapped Jordan for revenge. Maybe he was even working with someone else.

Although if he'd taken Jordan because of the money, why hadn't he asked for a ransom?

Everything was normal. He was eating and gaining weight. Although the doctor insisted he was too young to smile, he had smiled at her as she'd hugged him on the way back to the car.

Of course he'd had a fit when she put him in the car seat. Apparently he didn't like to be confined.

The bars on the cell mocked her. Neither did she.

She closed her eyes and saw his little face again. So trusting. So sweet and innocent. He'd smelled like baby wash. He had her blue eyes and a full head of light-colored hair.

At the doctor's office, two other mothers had commented on how beautiful he was. The nurse who'd delivered him, Amy Yost, had phoned to see how the checkup went. Tia had invited the young woman over for coffee the next day.

They'd chatted and become friends. Amy suggested she and her three-year-old daughter, Linnie, get together more often.

After Amy left, Tia's neighbor Judy Kinley had dropped by with brownies and a basket of goodies for Jordie—diaper wipes, baby washcloths, onesies and a blanket she'd crocheted herself.

Tia had enjoyed the visit but finally admitted that she needed a nap, that she'd been up half the night and maybe they could visit another day.

But none of those memories were helpful. She hadn't seen anyone lurking around the house watching her. No strangers had come to the door. She hadn't seen any cars following her. And she hadn't received any odd phone calls.

She closed her eyes and flopped back on the cot, her head spinning. Just as she was about to drift to sleep, the sound of a baby crying echoed in her ears.

She jerked upright in search of Jordie and

realized she was still in jail. Emotions racked her body.

She was no closer to finding her son than she had been the day before.

JUST AFTER DAWN, Ryder crawled from bed, irritated that he'd let thoughts of his conversation with Cash keep him awake. When he'd finally gotten the McCullens off his mind, Tia's big blue eyes had haunted him.

He showered and shaved, then dressed and strapped on his holster. He called Darren Hoyt on his way out the door.

"Meet me at the Sagebrush jail in half an hour. If you aren't there to file a report, I'll assume you're dropping the charges and I'll release Miss Jeffries."

He'd also fill Sheriff Gaines in on what he'd learned about Hoyt.

Then he wanted to search Tia's house himself. Maybe the sheriff had missed a clue.

Storm clouds hovered in the sky, painting the

woods a bleak gray and making the deserted land between his cabin and town look desolate. As he drove into town, he noted that the diner was already filling up with the breakfast crowd and several young mothers strolled their babies on the sidewalk and at the park while their toddlers and preschoolers ran and squealed on the playground.

He parked at the jail and went inside, his stomach clenching at the sight of another deputy at the desk. The old-timer had gray hair and a gut, and was slumped back in the chair, snoring like a bear.

Had he even checked on Tia?

Ryder rapped on the wooden desk. The man jumped, sending the chair backward with a thud as the edge hit the wall.

"Wha-what's going on?" The man fumbled with his wire-rimmed glasses.

Ryder identified himself. "I need to talk to Sheriff Gaines."

The man's face grew pinched as he adjusted his glasses. "This about the prisoner?"

"Yes," Ryder said between clenched teeth. "That and her missing child."

The man yawned. "Sheriff'll be in here soon. You can wait."

Ryder opened his mouth to ask him what he knew about the missing baby case, but the door swung open and Darren Hoyt barreled in. His clothes were disheveled, his eyes bloodshot and he reeked of whiskey.

"I'm here," Hoyt snapped. "Now let me sign those damn papers. I've got stuff to do."

Ryder grabbed the man by the collar and led him to the corner.

"Listen to me, you jerk. I did some digging on you last night and I know about your past."

"What are you talking about?" Hoyt growled. "I don't have a record."

"Not as Darren Hoyt, but you do under your real name."

Panic flared on Hoyt's face.

"Now, I suggest you tell me where Jordie Jeffries is."

"I told you last night, I don't know." He flung his hand toward the door leading to the cells. "Go ask my ex. She's the one that took the runt to her house."

Ryder jammed his face into the man's and gave him a warning look. "Because I don't believe she did anything but love that baby. You, on the other hand are a dirtbag of a father, a con man and a criminal."

Hoyt shook his head in denial. "That's not true—"

"Yes, it is," Ryder said coldly. "But if you confess and tell me where to find the baby, I'll go to bat for you with the judge."

"I don't know where he is," Darren screeched. "I swear I don't."

Ryder studied him for a long, frustrating minute. He wanted to beat the bastard until he confessed, but he couldn't do that here, not with that deputy watching.

"If that's true, prove it and drop the charges against Tia. The best way to find your son is for me to work with her."

Hoyt's breath rasped out. "You gonna watch her, see if she leads you to the baby?"

Ryder's gut tightened, but the lie came easy. "Exactly. You do want your son found unharmed, don't you?"

Hoyt's eyes darted toward the deputy, then the door opened and Sheriff Gaines strode in.

"What's going on?" the sheriff asked.

Ryder reluctantly released Hoyt. "Hoyt and I were just making a deal. He wants us to find his baby real bad."

The sheriff's eyebrows climbed his forehead as he jerked his head toward Hoyt. "That so?"

Hoyt nodded. Ryder patted his arm. "And you're dropping the charges against Miss Jeffries, right?"

Hoyt hissed a curse word, then gave another nod. "Just tell that crazy bitch not to come near me again."

Ryder barely resisted slugging the jerk. But he would keep Tia away from Hoyt for her own protection.

He gestured toward the deputy. “Please bring Miss Jeffries to the front.”

The older man ambled through the door, and Ryder turned to Gaines. “I need everything you have on this missing child case.”

“Wait just a damn minute,” Gaines said. “This is my jurisdiction.”

“Kidnapping is a federal offense. I’m officially taking over the case now.”

If he didn’t, Gaines would probably railroad Tia to prison and they’d never find her son.

Chapter Seven

Ryder watched as Hoyt stormed out the door. If the bastard cared about his baby, he'd be pushing him and the sheriff to find him.

Instead, Hoyt was more concerned with himself.

"Sheriff Gaines, did you search Tia's house after she reported her child missing?"

Gaines shifted, his chin set stubbornly. "Of course."

"What did you find?"

"Like I put in my report, the window was unlocked. No prints. No sign of foul play or that anyone had been in the house except Miss Jeffries."

"Can I see that report?"

Gaines shoved a file folder from his desk toward Ryder. Ryder quickly skimmed the notes on Tia's interview and photos of the empty crib and nursery.

"Did you take pictures when you searched the outer premises?"

Sheriff Gaines shook his head. "Wasn't nothing to photograph."

Ryder frowned. If an intruder had broken in, he would have expected to find something. Maybe footprints, brush disturbed.

He wanted to conduct his own search. "You can release her now."

The sheriff glared at him. "You sure that's a good idea?"

Ryder nodded. "Keep an open mind, Gaines. If Tia is innocent, whoever abducted her baby could be getting away."

FOOTSTEPS ON THE concrete floor startled Tia. What was going to happen now? Was the sheriff or that agent taking her to court for a bail hearing?

Had one of them found Jordie?

An older deputy appeared, his scowl menacing. Keys jangled as he unlocked the cell.

She rubbed her wrists. Even though the agent had removed the handcuffs, she could still feel the weight of the cold metal. Was he going to handcuff her again?

"Let's go," the deputy barked.

Tia inhaled a deep breath, stood and crossed the floor to the cell door. The deputy gestured for her to follow him, but he surprised her by not cuffing her. Exhaustion pulled at her, but she held her head high.

Darren had depleted her checking and savings. If she needed bail money, she could ask her assistant at Crossroads to dip into their funds to bail her out.

But that was a last resort.

Except for paying herself a small salary, she

never used the charity's money for personal reasons.

But if her parents had been alive, they'd agree that she should do anything to find her baby.

When the deputy opened the door to the front office, she blinked at how bright it seemed, a reminder that life in prison meant missing fresh air and sunshine.

A shadow caught her eye, then the figure came into focus. Agent Banks.

Her lungs squeezed for air. If he hadn't arrested her, she might find him attractive.

He *was* attractive. Tall, dark and handsome.

But he'd locked her up the night before and left her alone in jail when she should have been out looking for her baby.

RYDER SCRUTINIZED TIA to make certain she was okay. Leaving a woman alone in a jail with a male-only staff, especially with men he didn't know, always worried him.

She looked exhausted and frightened, but there

were no visible signs that she'd been abused or manhandled.

"What's going on?" she asked.

"Hoyt decided to drop the charges," Ryder said.

She glanced at the sheriff for confirmation.

"Guess it's your lucky day," the sheriff said in a voice harsh with displeasure. "But I suggest you stay away from your ex or you'll be right back here."

Tia gave a nod. "Do you have new information on my son?"

Gaines cut his eyes toward Ryder. "You'll have to ask him. It's his case now."

Another surprised look flitted across Tia's face, then relief. She obviously didn't trust Gaines to do his job.

Ryder gestured toward the door leading outside. "I'll drive you home."

Tia rubbed her hands up and down her arms as if she was trying to hold herself together as they crossed the room to the door.

"Don't leave town, Miss Jeffries," Gaines muttered.

She paused, animosity streaking her face. "I'm going to find my little boy," she said sharply.

Gaines started to say something else, but Ryder coaxed Tia out the door before they shared another exchange.

He placed his hand to Tia's back as they stepped onto the sidewalk and felt a shiver run through her.

"Are you all right?" he asked gruffly.

She shook her head. "I won't be all right until I'm holding Jordie again."

He understood that. "Let's talk at your house. I'm sure you want a shower and some food."

She didn't comment. She simply slid into the passenger seat of his SUV.

"I don't know how you convinced Darren to drop the charges, but I appreciate that."

He started the engine. "I don't like him," he said bluntly.

A small smile tugged at her mouth, making

him wish he could permanently wipe the anguish from her face. "You mean you saw through his act. Sheriff Gaines certainly seems to believe whatever Darren says."

"I know. I don't understand that." He gripped the steering wheel tighter, then veered onto the road leading to Tia's house.

She angled her head, her eyes narrowed. "How do you know where I live?"

He winced. "It's my job, Tia."

She heaved a breath. "You were watching me, weren't you? That's the reason you were at Darren's when I confronted him."

Confronted was putting it mildly. "Yes," he said, deciding to be straightforward. "Kidnapping and a missing baby warrant the feds' attention."

He pulled into the drive of the small bungalow. Flowers danced in the window boxes, the house was painted a soothing gray blue and a screened porch made it look homey—and totally at odds with Tia's current situation.

"Do you own or rent?" Ryder asked.

"I own it," Tia said. "I was living in an apartment before, but I wanted Jordie to have a real home with a yard to play in." Her voice broke. "I thought when he got older, we'd get a dog."

Ryder swallowed hard. There was no way this woman had hurt her child.

"I know Sheriff Gaines searched the house and property, but I intend to conduct my own search."

Ryder grabbed his kit from the trunk then followed Tia up to the front porch. She opened the door, and he followed her in.

Just as he'd expected, signs of a new baby were everywhere—a basket of baby clothes from the laundry. An infant bouncy seat. Toys scattered on a dinosaur blanket on the floor.

"The nursery is this way." Tia picked up a stuffed bear from the couch and hugged it to her as if she needed something in her arms to fill the void of her missing baby.

She led him across the den into a small hallway. A bathroom was situated between two bedrooms.

"Jordie's room is in here."

The moment he stepped inside the nursery, the love Tia had put into decorating the room engulfed him.

"Has anyone been inside the house since Jordie was born?" Ryder asked.

Tia rubbed her temple. "Elle and Ina dropped by and brought dinner and a basket of baby things."

"I spoke with them. They sang your praises." He paused, mentally eliminating them from his suspect list. He needed to look into the two people they'd suggested might hold a grudge against Tia.

"They're both wonderful and are godsends with the women and families who come through. I wish I could afford to pay them more, but they don't seem to mind."

"Who else?"

"A neighbor dropped by to bring me some treats and a gift for Jordie."

"Which neighbor?"

"Judy Kinley, the lady who lives behind me."

Ryder made a mental note to check her out. "Anyone else?"

She scrunched her mouth in thought. "Darren stopped by to drop off the finalized divorce decree."

He bit back a curse. "What a guy."

"I know. I was an idiot to ever believe he cared."

Ryder didn't comment. Men like Darren Hoyt were predators. He saw it all the time.

"I'm going to look around the room and check outside," he said instead.

Hopefully he'd find a clue that the sheriff had missed.

TIA DESPERATELY WANTED a shower, but she felt uncomfortable with the federal agent in the house, so she watched as he combed through the nursery.

"What are you looking for?" she asked.

"Fingerprints. Forensics that would prove someone broke in."

He dusted the crib and the windowsill for prints.

"Did you find anything?"

He shook his head. "Not yet. But the kidnapper could have worn gloves."

Because he'd planned this. But who would do such a thing? Darren was the only one who knew about her inheritance. And he hadn't asked for money. He'd denied knowing anything about the kidnapping, when in private he could have blackmailed her into paying.

Ryder examined the window lock, then knelt to check the floor below, then the wall. He removed a camera from his kit and took a picture.

"What do you see?" she asked.

"Scuff marks. It's not enough to cast, but it might be important."

He examined the lock again. "This definitely wasn't jimmied. Did someone else come in the house that day? Someone who might have unlocked the window without you being aware?"

Tia pressed two fingers to her temple as she mentally retraced her movements that day. "Judy came by and a friend I made at the hospital, my delivery nurse, Amy, stopped in with her little girl. We had coffee. Elle and Ina came later. They dropped off a casserole and saw Jordie for a minute. But none of them would have unlocked the window."

"I asked Elle and Ina about two people on your list, Wanda Hanson and a man, Bennett Jones. They mentioned they might hold a grudge against you."

"They were both angry," Tia said. "But I can't imagine either one of them kidnapping Jordie to get back at me."

"I want to talk to them anyway," Ryder said. "Sometimes people crack and do unexpected things."

She followed him outside to the back of the house, to the nursery window.

"Stay put," he said bluntly. "If there is something here, you don't want to contaminate it."

Tia wrung her hands together and hoped that he found something that would lead them to her baby.

RYDER CIRCLED THE house outside, searching the patches of grass and weeds. An area near the window looked as if the foliage had been mashed—as in footprints.

It could have happened when Gaines conducted his search, although the man obviously hadn't been very thorough. If he had, he would have photographed the window and surrounding area.

He snapped photos of his own, capturing the disturbed bushes and dirt. A partial shoe print was embedded in the ground, which at least suggested someone—a man?—had been outside the room.

That lent credence to Tia's story.

Of course, Gaines could argue that Tia had paid someone to take the baby.

He texted the tech team at the Bureau, instructing them to check Tia's financials for anything suspicious, and also to look into Wanda Hanson and Bennett Jones.

He peered closer and discovered smudges on the wood beneath the window frame. Another partial boot print where the intruder had climbed onto the ledge and slipped through the window. He snapped pictures of the ledge, noting broken splinters around the edge and smudges on the windowpane.

He studied it for a print, but the kidnapper must have worn gloves, as there was no clear print.

Something caught his eye below, wedged into the weeds, and he stooped and combed through the area.

A pack of matches, with a logo for the Big Mug.

He hadn't seen ashtrays or any evidence that Tia was a smoker in her house.

His pulse kicked up. The matches could have belonged to the person who'd taken her son.

Chapter Eight

Still grungy from the jail cell, Tia stepped onto the porch for air. When she'd first bought the house, she'd imagined rocking Jordan out here on cool spring and fall nights, doing artwork with him as he grew older and adding a swing set to the backyard.

She blinked back more tears, then spotted Judy, the neighbor whose house backed up to Tia's, standing on her deck. She was peering at Tia's house through binoculars.

Ryder stepped onto the porch, his phone in hand. "Who's the woman with the binoculars?"

"That's Judy Kinley."

"Tell me about her."

Tia bit her lower lip. "She seems friendly, although she's a little nosy. She works at home doing accounting for a couple of small businesses."

"Married? Kids?"

"No." Tia shook her head. "At first I thought it was comforting to have a neighbor close by, in case of an emergency, one who'd watch out for my property, but she tends to just drop by. I guess she's lonely."

Agent Banks arched a brow. "She comes by a lot?"

Tia shrugged. "A few times. Once she brought cookies and another time a pie. Apparently she likes to bake."

"Did she know your ex?"

"No," Tia said. "I wanted a fresh start, so I moved here after he and I split up."

He nodded. "Is she always peering at the neighbors?"

Tia tucked a strand of hair behind her ear. "She started a community watch program."

"Was she home the night Jordie disappeared?"

"Yes," Tia said. "When I found his crib empty, I called the sheriff. A few minutes after he arrived, Judy rushed over to see what was wrong and what she could do to help."

An odd expression flickered in Ryder's eyes. "I'm going to talk to her. I also want to speak to some of your other neighbors. Maybe one of them saw something."

Although if so, why hadn't he or she come forward?

RYAN CROSSED TIA'S BACKYARD, then strode toward the neighbor's back deck. He waved his identification. "Ma'am, my name is Special Agent Ryder Banks. I'd like to ask you some questions."

She lowered the binoculars and stepped back as if startled. Ryder paused at the bottom of the steps, studying her. She was probably in her early forties, with a face already weathered from too much sun. A few strands of gray hair mingled with the muddy brown, and she wore a drab T-shirt and jeans that hung on her thin frame.

"Tia said your name is Judy. Is that right?"

"Yes. I assume you're investigating the disappearance of her baby."

Ryder nodded. "Yes, ma'am. May I come up and talk to you for a few minutes?"

She clenched the binoculars by her side. "I don't know how I can help, but sure, come on up."

Ryder wasn't buying the innocent act. Anyone who watched their neighbors through binoculars knew what was going on in the neighborhood.

His footsteps pounded the wooden steps as he climbed them.

"Can I get you some lemonade or tea?" Judy asked.

"No, thanks." He gestured toward Tia's house and saw her watching. "How well do you know Tia Jeffries?"

Judy shrugged and leaned against the deck railing. "We've chatted a few times."

"You were living here when she moved in?"

"No, I moved in after her. My husband passed away and I wanted to downsize."

"Tell me what you know about Tia."

Judy fluttered her fingers through her short hair. "Tia seems like a nice young woman. She was alone, too, so I introduced myself."

"Did you meet her ex-husband?"

Judy pursed her lips. "No, I can't say I wanted to, either. Any man who'd abandon his pregnant wife is pretty low in my book."

He agreed. "Tia said you started a neighborhood watch program. You were also home the night her baby disappeared. Did you notice any strangers lurking around? A car that was out of place?"

She shook her head no. "Although Darren stopped by, Tia said he brought the divorce papers."

"Was she upset about that?"

"No, she seemed relieved it would be final."

Ryder shifted. Darren could have slipped into the nursery and unlocked the window without Tia's knowledge.

"Tell me about the night the baby went missing."

"What do you mean?"

"Tia said she'd fallen asleep and when she woke up and checked on the baby, he was gone. She called 911, then you came over when you saw the police."

"That's right."

"How was she?" Ryder asked.

"How do you think she was?" Judy said with a bite to her tone. "Someone kidnapped her child. She was hysterical."

"What exactly did she say?"

"She was crying so hard she could barely talk." Judy sighed wearily. "But she said someone had kidnapped Jordan from his bed. I tried to calm Tia while the sheriff searched the house and outside."

"Did Tia say anything else?"

Judy rubbed her forehead. "She just kept begging the sheriff to find her son. He asked about her marriage. She told him about the divorce, then she said she was afraid Darren abducted the infant."

"According to Tia, he left her because she refused to give him money from her charity."

"True." Judy made a low sound in her throat. "But if he took the little boy for money, why hasn't he demanded a ransom?"

Good question. And one Ryder wanted the answer to.

UNABLE TO BEAR the scent of her clothes any longer, Tia stripped and stepped into the shower. The hot water felt wonderful, but as she closed her eyes, images of her little boy taunted her.

"I promise I'll find you," she whispered. "I will bring you home and I'll never let you out of my sight again."

She scrubbed her body three times to cleanse

the ugliness of the jail cell, then soaped and rinsed her hair. When she climbed out, she brushed her teeth, pulled on a clean T-shirt and pair of jeans, and dried her hair.

The agent still hadn't returned.

The hole in her heart continued to ache, and she stepped back into the nursery and ran her fingers over the baby quilt she'd hand sewn. Each square featured an appliqué, a hodgepodge of different breeds of puppies. She'd imagined naming the dogs on the quilt with Jordie. And when he was older, they'd visit the animal shelter and choose a dog to adopt.

She'd painted the room a bright blue and his dresser a barnyard red. She opened up one of the drawers and touched the sleepers she'd neatly folded, the tiny bootees and socks, then hugged the little knit cap he'd worn home from the hospital to her chest. She blinked back more tears as she inhaled Jordie's newborn scent.

She had to do something to find her son.

Maybe a personal plea on the news.

She'd talk to that agent when he returned.

If he didn't agree, she'd find a way to do it herself.

RYDER CANVASSED THE NEIGHBORHOOD, but no one had seen or heard anything suspicious the night before or the night of Jordie's disappearance. Several of them hadn't even met Tia, as she'd only moved in a few weeks before.

Two older women claimed they'd seen Tia strolling the baby in the mornings. She'd looked tired but doted on her child.

He walked back to Tia's, frustrated that he hadn't discovered anything helpful.

On a positive note, he hadn't heard anything derogatory about Tia, nothing to make him doubt her story.

He banged the horse door knocker, and Tia opened the door. She'd showered, and her hair looked damp as it hung around her shoulders.

His gut tightened. She was damn gorgeous.

Not something he should be noticing or thinking about.

"Did you learn anything?" Tia asked.

He shook his head. "Afraid not. None of your neighbors seemed suspicious, but I'm going to run background checks on each of them just to be on the safe side. I want to talk to the hospital staff next."

Tia frowned. "Why? Jordie was taken from my house."

"I know. But we have to consider every possibility. Perhaps a stranger or another patient was in the hospital looking at the babies, someone who didn't belong."

Tia's eyes widened. "You mean someone could have been watching Jordie, looking for a chance to take him?"

Ryder shrugged. "Either him or another child. We could be dealing with a desperate, possibly unstable parent. Perhaps someone who lost a child or couldn't have a baby was depressed, desperate. He or she could have scouted out the nursery. It's happened before."

Tia shivered.

Ryder couldn't resist. He gently took her arms in his hands and forced her to face him. "If someone took him because they wanted a family, that means Jordie will be well taken care of, that he or she will keep him safe."

Tia released a pent-up breath, then gave a little nod. "I want to appear on television and make a plea for whoever took Jordie to return him to me."

Ryder hesitated. "That could work, but it could backfire, Tia. Sometimes going to the media draws out the crazies and we waste time on false leads."

Her eyes glittered with emotions. "Maybe. But if the person who abducted Jordie wants a family like you suggested, seeing how much I love and miss my baby might make them rethink what they've done and bring him back."

He couldn't argue with that.

"Please, Agent Banks," she whispered. "I have to do everything I can to find him."

Ryder inhaled. "All right, I'll set it up."

"For today," Tia said. "I want to do it right away."

"All right, but call me Ryder." After all, they were going to be spending a lot of time together—as much as it took until they recovered her son.

"All right, Ryder," she said, her soft voice filled with conviction. "I want to speak to the press as soon as possible."

Ryder nodded then stepped aside to make the call.

TIA'S HEART RACED as Ryder returned, his phone in hand. "Did you set it up?"

"Yes. At six. They'll air it on the evening news."

"Good. That will give us time to go to the hospital."

Ryder agreed and they hurried to his SUV.

Ten minutes later, she led the way to the hospital maternity floor. The nurses at the nurses' station looked surprised to see Tia, their nervous whispers making her wonder what they thought.

Hilda, the head charge nurse, hurried around the desk edge and swept her into a hug. "Oh, my God, Tia. I'm so sorry about the kidnapping. Did the police find Jordie?"

Tia shook her head no and introduced Ryder. "Agent Banks is looking for him."

"I need to talk to each of the staff members who were on duty the night Tia delivered."

Hilda looked eager to help. "All right, I'll get a list and text them."

"Also, I need to know if anyone suspicious has been lurking around the nursery area and this ward."

"Not that I know of," Hilda said. "But I'll ask around."

"Do you have security cameras on this floor?"

"Absolutely," Hilda said. "We take our patients' and their children's safety very seriously."

"Good. I want to review all the tapes the week prior to Jordie's disappearance as well as the week he was born."

Hilda nodded, then stepped to the desk to set things up.

Tia held her breath. If Ryder was right, maybe the person who'd taken her son was on one of those tapes.

Chapter Nine

Tia hurried toward the nurse who'd coached her during labor. Amy spoke to her, then Tia introduced Ryder.

"This is Special Agent Ryder Banks," Tia said. "He's helping me search for my son."

Ryder flashed his credentials. "I'm talking to all the staff," he said. "You were here the night Tia delivered her son?"

Amy nodded. "I worked night shift that week."

Tia offered her a smile of gratitude. "Amy was my labor coach. I couldn't have done it without her."

Amy shrugged. "You did the hard work, Tia."

Her voice cracked. "I'm just sorry for what's happened."

Tia swallowed the fear eating at her. "I'm going on television to make a plea to get Jordie back."

Amy squeezed her hand. "I hope that helps."

Ryder cleared his throat. "Amy, have you noticed anyone lurking around the maternity floor? Maybe someone near the nursery?"

Amy fidgeted with the pocket of her uniform. "Not really."

"How about a patient who lost a child?" Cash's story about the McCullens echoed in his head. "A grieving mother might be desperate enough to take someone else's child to fill the void of her own loss."

Amy squeezed Tia's hand again. "That's true. But I can't discuss other patients' medical charts or history."

"You don't have to. Just tell me if there's someone who fits that description."

Amy worried her bottom lip with her teeth.

"There was one woman who suffered from complications and delivered prematurely, only twenty weeks."

Tia's heart ached for her. "That must have been devastating."

Amy nodded. "She and her husband were in the middle of a divorce, so she blamed him. She thought the stress triggered her premature labor."

Hilda returned and motioned for them to join her at the desk. "The security guard is waiting whenever you want to take a look at those tapes."

"Thanks." Ryder turned back to Amy. "Why don't you watch the tapes with us? If you see anyone you think is suspicious, you can point them out."

Amy and Hilda exchanged concerned looks, then Amy followed them to the security office. They passed a nurse named Richard who grunted hello.

Amy exchanged a smile with him and introduced Ryder. “I’m canvassing the staff to see if anyone saw or heard anything strange when Miss Jeffries was here.”

“I didn’t see anyone suspicious.” Richard gave Tia a sympathetic look. “I’m sorry about your baby, Miss Jeffries.”

Tia murmured thanks, then Richard had to go to the ER.

Hilda led them into the security room, and she, Ryder and Amy gathered to view the tapes.

When the guard zeroed in on the camera feed showing her at admissions, Tia’s heart gave a painful tug. That night she’d been so excited. After nine months of carrying her baby inside her, of feeling his little feet and fists push at her belly, of listening to his heartbeat during the ultrasounds and imagining what he might look like, her son was going to be born.

She was going to have a family of her own.

He had cried the moment he’d come out, a beautiful sound that had brought tears to her eyes. He had a cap of light blond hair, blue eyes and tiny pink fingers that had grasped her finger when she'd caressed him to her breast.

But now he was gone.

RYDER PARKED HIMSELF in front of the security feed, anxious to find a lead. Amy certainly seemed to care about Tia and wanted to be helpful.

Tia's breath rattled out with nerves as she sank into the chair beside him. One camera shot captured her entering the ER—apparently she'd driven herself. She held her bulging belly with one hand, breathing deeply, as she handled the paperwork.

Although her hair was pulled back in a ponytail and she was obviously in pain, she looked... happy. Glowing with the kind of joy an expectant mother should be feeling.

All his life, he'd thought his birth mother had sold him. But if Cash was telling the truth, she hadn't done any such thing.

She died trying to find us.

Cash had insisted that was the truth.

Had his biological mother felt that anticipation over giving birth to him and Cash, only to be grief stricken when she was told her twins were stillborn?

His lungs squeezed for air. How she must have suffered.

Tia was wheeled into a triage room, then a delivery room, where they lost sight of her.

"Let's look at the hallways near the nursery the week before—"

"Go back to the day he was born," Amy suggested quietly.

That must have been around the time when the other woman lost her baby.

The next half hour they studied each section of the tape, zeroing in on parents and grandparents and friends who'd visited—most of whom looked elated as they oohed and aahed over the infants in the nursery.

Couples came and went, huddling together,

smiling, laughing and crying as they watched the newborns.

Emotions churned in Ryder's belly. He'd never imagined having a family of his own—a wife, kids. Not in the picture. Not with the job he did.

A long empty space of tape, then another crew of family members appeared, gushing and waving through the glass window.

Just as they left, a young woman emerged from the shadows, her thin face haggard and lined with fatigue. She was hunched inside an oversize raincoat, her hair pulled back beneath a scarf, her face a picture of agony as she studied the infants. The nurse, Richard Blotter, paused as he passed, his gaze narrowed.

"There's Jordie," Tia said in a raw whisper.

The woman hesitated as she walked along the window, eyeing the pink and blue bundles. She paused in front of Jordie's bassinet.

Tia straightened, her body tensing as she leaned forward to home in on the woman's face.

"She's looking at Jordie," she said in a low voice.

Yes, she was.

Richard passed the nursery, but the woman hurried away.

Ryder swung his gaze toward Amy, but she quickly glanced toward the floor, avoiding eye contact as she bit her lower lip.

"Do you know who this woman is?" Ryder asked.

"I don't remember her name," Amy said, "but she's the woman I mentioned who lost her baby."

"I need a copy of this tape," he told the security guard.

The tech team could work wonders with facial recognition software. He'd also get a warrant for medical records and find out her name.

She might be the person who'd stolen Tia's child.

TIA CONSTANTLY CHECKED the clock as Ryder questioned other staff members. Hilda discreetly ran a check for any patients who'd required mental health services.

As they left the hospital, Ryder drove to the county crime lab and dropped off the partial print and matches he'd found outside the nursery along with the tapes for analysis. He wanted the ID of the woman who'd been watching those babies.

He received a text from the FBI analyst as they walked back to his SUV. "One of our analysts located Bennett Jones."

"Where is he?"

"Jones remarried and moved to Texas. Been there four months. His first wife claims he's made no move to see their baby since he met the other woman."

Tia gritted her teeth. "That's not uncommon. He was angry when she left, had a bruised ego, but he quickly replaced his family with another one."

Ryder grunted a sound of disapproval. "I also have an address for the woman, Wanda Hanson.

She entered a rehab program after her husband gained custody of their infant."

"Where is she now?"

"A few miles outside Pistol Whip." He started the engine and pulled onto the highway. Tia contemplated the woman in the security tape as he drove. Sympathy for her situation and her loss filled Tia. If she'd taken Jordie, hopefully he was in good hands.

But Jordie belonged to her. *With* her.

And she would do whatever necessary to bring him home.

The sun dipped behind a sea of dark clouds, painting the sky a dismal gray. The farmland looked desolate, with dry scrub brush dotting the landscape, the ground thirsty for water.

Ryder drove down a narrow two-lane road past a cluster of small, older homes that needed serious upkeep. A few toys and bicycles were scattered around, the yards overgrown and full of weeds.

He checked his phone for the address, then

turned in the drive of a redbrick ranch. Anxious to see if Wanda had her son, Tia slipped from the vehicle and started up the drive. Ryder caught her before she made it to the front door.

"Let me handle this," Ryder said in a gruff voice.

"She hates me, Ryder. If she took Jordie, the minute she sees me, she'll know the reason I'm here."

And Tia would know by the look on Wanda's face if she was guilty.

RYDER PUNCHED THE DOORBELL, his gaze scanning the property for any sign Wanda was home, but there was no car in the drive. It was impossible to see in the tiny windowless garage.

Tia stepped slightly to the right and peered through the front window. From his vantage point, the house looked dark.

"Do you see anything? Any movement?" he asked.

"No one in the kitchen or den."

He rang the bell again, then banged on the door. Seconds passed with no response. He jiggled the doorknob, but it was locked.

"I'm going to check around the side and back."

He veered to the left and Tia followed.

"You're sure this is her place?" Tia asked.

"Yes, our analyst, Gwen, is good at her job. Apparently Wanda had no money for rent or to buy a house. This place belonged to her mother, who passed away last year. She's been living here since the custody hearing."

He passed the side window. No lights inside. The curtains hung askew, clothes scattered around the room. Dry leaves crunched as they inched to the back door. He jiggled the door but it was locked.

Dammit, he wanted to search the interior. He removed a tiny tool from his pocket just as Tia did the same.

"I've got it," he said, remembering the way they'd met. "Don't touch anything, Tia. If we find evidence, I don't want it thrown out because you were present."

"Don't you need a warrant?" Her brows furrowed at the unpleasant reminder, and she jammed the tool back in her pocket.

Hell, he was breaking the rules. "Technically, yes. But it's acceptable if I have probable cause. I can always say we heard a noise and thought the baby was inside."

Ryder yanked on latex gloves, opened the door, flipped on the overhead light and called out, "FBI Special Agent Banks. Is anyone here?"

Silence echoed back. Then Ryder stepped into the tiny kitchen. Outdated appliances, linoleum and a rickety table made the room look fifty years old. A dirty coffee cup sat in the sink along with a plate of dried, molded food. The garbage reeked as if it hadn't been taken out in days.

Ryder opened the refrigerator, and Tia spotted a carton of milk, eggs, condiments and a jar of applesauce.

On the second shelf sat two baby bottles, half full of formula.

Her pulse jumped. Why would Wanda have baby formula and bottles when there were no kids in the house?

Her child was a toddler, too, not a baby, so why the bottle?

Ryder crossed the room into the den and flipped on a lamp. The soft light illuminated the room just enough for her to see that Wanda wasn't a housekeeper.

Magazines, dirty laundry and mail were spread across the couch and table. A worn teddy bear had been stuffed in the corner along with an infant's receiving blanket.

Tia followed Ryder into the hall. The first bedroom had been turned into a nursery. Tia scanned the room, her heart racing at the sight of a tiny bassinet.

Wanda's baby had long ago outgrown it, but a receiving blanket lay inside, along with an elephant-shaped blue rattle.

A baby had been here recently. Was it Jordie?

Ryder paused to look at it, then walked over to the changing table and lifted the lid on the diaper pail.

"Was Wanda allowed visitation rights?" Tia asked.

He shrugged, then made a quick phone call and identified himself. "Mr. Hanson, was your wife allowed visitation rights to your child?"

Tia held her breath while she waited for the answer.

"No. Hmm," Ryder mumbled. Another pause. "When did you last see her or speak with her?"

Silence stretched for a full minute. Ryder thanked the man then his gaze darkened.

"He hasn't heard from her. Said she hasn't seen the kid, but he's safe with him. The last time he talked to her, she'd fallen off the wagon and screamed at him that she hadn't deserved to lose her little boy."

Tia trembled. Wanda blamed her, not her drug addiction.

Ryder opened the dresser drawer—several baby outfits, all for newborn three-month-old boys. He hurried to the next bedroom while she stood stunned at the sight of the clothes.

Ryder's gruff voice made her stomach clench. "It looks as if her suitcase is gone and her clothes have been cleaned out, like she left in a hurry."

Tia gripped the edge of the baby bed. Had Wanda abducted Jordie and gone on the run?

Chapter Ten

Fear paralyzed Tia. "Look at these clothes and baby things," she said to Ryder. "If Wanda has Jordie, with the border less than a day's drive away, she might have taken him out of the country."

Ryder snatched his phone from the belt at his waist. "I'm going to issue a BOLO for her. Do you know what kind of car she drives?"

Tia searched her memory banks. "She used to drive a black Honda, but that's been over a year or so."

"I'll have Gwen check her out. Look through that basket on the kitchen counter. See if you find a pay stub or anything else that might indicate where she's going."

He riffled through the desk in the corner as he phoned the Bureau.

She focused on the basket. Piles of overdue bills, a lottery ticket, a speeding ticket that hadn't been paid, a letter from the rehab center asking her to call her counselor.

A manila envelope lay beside the basket. Tia opened it as Ryder stepped back into the room. She sighed at the legal document granting custody of Wanda's child to her husband.

She dug deeper and discovered a pack of matches.

Her heart thumped wildly. The logo on the outside read the Big Mug.

The same logo was on the matches Ryder had found in the bushes outside her baby's nursery. "Look at these."

"We need to stop by that bar," Ryder said. "I sent those other matches to the lab for prints.

I'll do the same with these and see if they have the same prints."

Hope flared in Tia's chest. "If the prints match, that means Wanda took Jordie."

"Don't jump the gun," Ryder said. "Let's canvass the neighbors and see if anyone noticed Wanda acting strangely or if they saw her with an infant."

He gestured to the laundry basket. "Look through those clothes and the laundry and see if any of the baby things are familiar. What was Jordie wearing the night he was abducted?"

The memory of that baby sleeper haunted her. "A light blue sleeper with an appliqué of a wagon and horse." She rushed toward the laundry piled on the couch.

An assortment of receiving blankets, caps, outfits, bootees and…a sleeper. She quickly examined it. No appliqué of a wagon and horse—a teddy bear instead. She frantically searched the rest of the laundry, but the sleeper wasn't there.

Relief mingled with worry. She didn't want to

think that Wanda had taken Jordie because she was angry. If the woman was drinking or taking pills again, she might have an accident or hurt him.

No. She had to remain optimistic. She closed her eyes and said a silent prayer that Jordie was safe.

Ryder touched her elbow. "Gwen is alerting airports, train stations and bus stations to watch for Wanda. She's sent photos of Jordie and Wanda nationwide. If they try to get out of the country, we'll stop them."

"I hope so," Tia said.

Ryder took another look through the house while she checked the chest in the nursery.

Ten minutes later, they walked to the neighbor's house next door. A tiny gray-haired woman opened the door, leaning on a cane.

Ryder identified himself, flashed his credentials, then explained the reason for their visit.

"I'm Myrtle." The little woman gave Tia a sympathetic smile. "I'm sorry about your baby, miss. People coming in your house and stealing your children—I don't know what the world is coming to. It's just plain awful."

Ryder cleared his throat. "When did you last see your neighbor Wanda?"

"About three days ago," Myrtle said.

"You mean Wednesday?" Ryder asked.

Myrtle nodded. "Early that morning, I saw her carrying some kind of bundle out to the car. Then she sped away."

Tia's lungs squeezed for air. Tuesday night was when Jordie disappeared.

RYDER AND TIA spent the next half hour questioning other neighbors. They met a young woman strolling twin toddlers into the driveway across the street. Tia gushed over the children, a boy and girl, who looked to be about a year and a half old.

Ryder made the introductions.

"I'm Dannika," the young woman said. "I'm not sure how I can help."

"Tell us about your neighbor Wanda," Ryder began.

Dannika claimed Wanda liked to entertain late at night, and that she'd seen several men come and go over the last month but had never been introduced to any of them. One drove a black Range Rover and another a dented white pickup. She made sure her children stayed in the fenced backyard instead of wondering to the front because she was worried about Wanda's driving.

Tia's face blanched at that statement.

Ryder didn't like the picture this neighbor was painting. "She was driving while intoxicated?"

"It appeared that way," the young woman said. "She was reckless, weaving all over the road. One night she smashed her own mailbox."

Tia wiped perspiration from her forehead. "Did she have family around?"

"Not that I know of."

"Did you see her with a baby?" Ryder asked.

The woman took a sip of her bottled water. "No, although sometime Wednesday afternoon, she was carrying a bundle to the car. It could have been a baby wrapped up in a blanket."

Ryder's jaw hardened, but he worked to maintain a neutral expression. So if she'd left early that morning, she might have returned for some reason. "Was anyone with her that day?"

"No. But an SUV was parked in the drive that morning."

"What kind?"

She rubbed her forehead. "Black. I think it was a 4Runner."

"Did you see the driver?"

She shook her head. "I'm afraid not. I didn't think much of it at the time."

Ryder handed her a business card. "If you think of anything else that might help, please give me a call."

She accepted the card with a nod then knelt to console the little girl who'd woken from her nap and started to fuss.

Tia looked longingly at the toddlers as they said goodbye and walked to the next house.

A teenage boy answered the door wearing a rock band T-shirt, his arms covered in tattoos, a cigarette dangling from the corner of his mouth. His eyes looked bloodshot. “Yeah?”

“Are your parents home?” Ryder asked.

The kid’s fingers curled around the door edge as if he might slam it in their face—or run. “No.”

“Where are they?”

“Daddy lit out when I was three. Mama’s working at the dry cleaner’s down the street.” He shoved his hand in his back pocket and shifted nervously. “Why?”

“I need to talk to them.”

Panic streaked the teen’s eyes when Ryder flashed his badge. “Look, man, I ain’t done nothing.”

Ryder chuckled sarcastically. “I don’t care if you’re smoking weed or have drugs here at the moment, buddy. We’re looking for a kidnapped baby.”

The teen cursed. “I didn’t steal any kid.”

“It was my baby,” Tia said quickly. “And we

don't think you took him. But the woman next door, Wanda, might have."

"Have you seen her around?" Ryder asked.

The boy tugged at the ripped end of his T-shirt. "Not today."

"Did you see her with a baby?" Tia asked.

"Naw." He shot a quick glance down the street.

"What's going on down there?" Ryder asked.

The boy looked down at his shoes. "That's where she gets her stash."

"Her dealer lives on the street?" Ryder asked.

The boy shrugged.

"Is he your supplier?" Ryder asked.

"No, hell, no." Fear darkened his face. "And don't tell him I said anything. I don't want him coming after me."

Ryder grimaced. "Don't worry, I won't mention you. I'll tell him we're talking to all the neighbors, which is true."

Relief softened the wariness in the teen's eyes.

Ryder pushed his card into the boy's hand.

"Call me if you see Wanda come back, or if you think of anything that could help."

The boy nodded, his eyes darting down the street again.

Ryder turned to leave, his gaze scanning the area in case someone was watching.

PURE PANIC SEIZED TIA. "Oh, my God," Tia said as the young man closed the door in their faces. "What if Wanda is high and driving around with Jordie? She might have an accident or lose her temper—"

"Shh, don't go there," he said softly. Ryder gripped Tia's arms and forced her to look at him. "We don't know that she took Jordie."

"But what if she did?" Tia cried. "I've heard of desperate addicts actually selling their children or trading them for their fix."

"I know it's difficult not to imagine the worst," Ryder said, "but we need to focus. We still have a lot of possibilities to explore. The woman in the security footage at the hospital, for one."

Tia inhaled a deep breath. "All right. What do we do next?"

"I'm going to talk to the drug dealer," Ryder said. "You need to wait in the car."

"But I want to hear what he has to say."

Ryder's jaw tightened. "It's too dangerous. We have no idea if he's armed or if there are thugs working with him."

He walked her back to his SUV.

"Be careful," Tia said as he started down the sidewalk toward the drug dealer's house.

She accessed the pictures on her phone and studied each one she'd taken of Jordie while she waited. Although she didn't need to look at them—she'd already memorized each detail.

RYDER SCRUTINIZED THE yard and house as he approached. The windows were covered with black-out curtains, the window in the garage covered as well.

Could be a sign that the man who lived inside had something to hide.

He raised his fist to knock, his instincts on alert. The yard was unkempt, and a black sedan with tinted windows sat in the drive. He banged his fist on the door, one hand sliding inside his jacket, ready to draw his weapon if needed.

Inside, a voice shouted something, then footsteps pounded.

Ryder knocked again, and the voice he'd heard called out, "Coming."

Ryder glanced to the side of house, looking for signs of a meth lab—or a runner.

The door squeaked open, and gray eyes peered back, a twentysomething male with a head of shaggy hair glaring at him. "Yeah?"

Ryder flashed his credentials and was rewarded by a panicked look from the guy. "I'm canvassing the neighbors to see if anyone has seen Wanda Hanson, who lives in that house." He pointed to the run-down ranch they'd come from.

"Listen, man, I don't know many of the neighbors," the guy said. "We don't exactly have cul-de-sac parties around here."

No, but maybe crack parties. "But you may have seen the news about a missing infant, a six-week-old boy named Jordie Jeffries?"

"Do I look like I've got a kid in here?" the guy said, belligerence edging his tone.

Suddenly a movement to the right caught Ryder's eye, then the door slammed shut in his face.

A second guy exited a side door and darted to a truck parked at the curb.

Ryder pulled his gun from his holster and shouted for him to stop. But the man he'd been talking to at the door ran out the side after the truck.

Suddenly Tia bolted from the SUV and dashed toward the truck.

He yelled for her to go back, but a shot rang out, the bullet zinging toward Tia.

Chapter Eleven

Ryder grabbed Tia and wrapped his arms around her, then threw her to the ground, using his body as a shield to protect her as they dodged another bullet.

Tia screamed and clutched his back as he rolled them toward the bushes.

"Stay down," he growled in her ear.

She nodded against his chest, and he lifted his head and peered up at the truck. Another bullet flew toward them.

He motioned for Tia to keep cover in the bushes as he drew his gun and fired at the driver. He missed and the man jumped in the truck.

Ryder pushed to his knees and inched forward, gun at the ready. The engine fired up. Tires squealed as the driver accelerated and pulled from the curb. Ryder jogged forward and shot at the tires, memorizing the tag as the truck sped down the road.

He turned and saw Tia running toward him. Dammit. "I told you to stay down."

"They're getting away," Tia cried.

Ryder stowed his gun in his holster and coaxed Tia back to his SUV. She sank into the passenger seat, and he phoned his superior and explained the situation, then gave him the license plate and the address of the house. "Get an APB out on this truck. I also need a warrant to search his place."

"You got it. I'll contact the local sheriff and have him bring the warrant."

Ryder bit the inside of his cheek. He didn't particularly want Sheriff Gaines in the middle of this, but excluding him would cause more trouble. Pissing off the man in his own jurisdiction could work against him.

Connor transferred him to the tech analyst Gwen.

Ryder gave her the home address. "Tell me what you find on the man who lives here."

Tia tucked a strand of hair behind her ear, her hand trembling. He tilted her chin up with his thumb. "You okay?"

She nodded, expression earnest as they waited.

Seconds later, Gwen came back on the phone. "House is owned by a couple in Texas. They've been renting it for the last year to a twenty-five-year-old student named Neil Blount. But…" She hesitated and Ryder thumped his boot on the ground.

"Arrest record?"

"A couple of misdemeanors for possession. Looks like he dropped out of college."

"Job history?"

"Nothing substantial. He worked at a couple

of hamburger joints. Last job was at a bar called the Big Mug."

Ryder hissed. The matches outside Tia's place had come from that bar. "Find out everything you can on that bar, its owner and history. They could be running drugs out of there."

TIA WATCHED AS Ryder and the sheriff entered Neil Blount's house. If Jordie had been with those men at any time, what had they done with him?

Her phone buzzed, the caller display box reading Crossroads.

It was Elle. "Hey, Tia, I just called to see how things are going."

Tia relayed what had happened. "At this point, I don't know if Wanda or this man had anything to do with Jordie's disappearance, but Ryder is looking into them. What's happening at Crossroads? Do you need me to come in?" Tia asked.

"No, everything is going smoothly," Elle assured her. "The new family has settled in. I already set up a job interview for the mother. She seems anxious to accept our help so she can get back on her feet."

"Good. That's half the battle," Tia murmured. Sometimes families resisted accepting help or, in some instances, emotional issues and addictions kept them from following through on good intentions.

"I'm saying a prayer for you," Elle said. "I know you're going to find him, Tia. I just know it."

Tia wished she felt as optimistic.

"Call me if you hear something."

Tia thanked her and disconnected just as Ryder exited the house. She rushed toward him. "Any sign of Jordie?"

He shook his head. "No. We did find drugs, enough to indicate Blount is into dealing bigtime. Sheriff Gaines agreed to get his deputy to work with one of the DEA's special agents to see just how big his operation is."

"Where is my baby, Ryder?" Tia said in a hoarse whisper.

Ryder wanted to console her, but he couldn't lie to her. "I found a laptop and am sending it to the lab for analysis. If there's any mention of a kidnapping or possible child-stealing ring, they'll find it."

Tia nodded, although anxiety knotted her shoulders. A child-stealing ring? God…that could mean that whoever had taken Jordie might have sold him to a stranger.

That stranger could be halfway across the world with her son by now.

RYDER HATED CHASING false leads, and Blount and Wanda both might be dead ends. Although at this point, he had no other clues. "We have time before the interview," Ryder said as he and Tia got in his SUV. "I want to go by the Big Mug on the way."

Tia twined her hands in her lap, twisting them

in a nervous gesture. "What if they're long gone? Maybe in Mexico or Europe or Brazil?"

Ryder covered her hand with his to calm her. Her fingers felt cold, stiff, her anxiety palpable. "That would mean passports, flight plans. We didn't find anything in Wanda's house to indicate she'd made arrangements to leave the country. And with the Amber Alert and airport, train and bus stations on guard, someone would have seen them."

"Not necessarily," Tia argued. "A woman cuddling a baby wouldn't arouse suspicion."

"No, but authorities will be watching for anyone behaving suspiciously. Also, to travel with an infant, you have to provide a birth certificate."

Ryder started the engine and pulled onto the road, heading toward the Big Mug.

"Can't people fake birth certificates?" Tia asked.

Ryder veered around a curve, staying right when the road forked. It definitely had happened, especially with criminals who stole children as a business. But he didn't want to panic Tia any more than she already was.

"It's difficult, but it can be done," Ryder said. "Knowing there's an Amber Alert for an infant, security personnel and authorities will scrutinize documents carefully." At least he hoped they would.

A slacker could miss crucial signs on faked documents, though. Worse, if the kidnapper was smart, he or she might have altered the baby's name, birth date and even his sex. People were looking for a baby boy. They might not take a second look at an infant swaddled in pink.

Tia lapsed into a strained silence while they drove, the deserted land stretching before them a reminder that a kidnapper could have vanished somewhere in the Wyoming wilderness and stay hidden until the hype surrounding the baby's disappearance died down.

Then he or she would try to make a hasty escape.

They had to find Jordie before that happened.

The gray clouds overhead darkened, casting a dismal feel as they ventured into the outskirts of town. The Big Mug sat off the country road next to a rustic-looking barbecue place called the Tasty Pig, a place Ryder had heard had the best barbecue this side of Cheyenne. His mouth watered at the thought, but one peek at Tia told him that food wasn't on her mind.

All she wanted was to find her baby. He didn't have time to feed his stomach when she was hurting and Jordie's kidnapper might be getting farther and farther away.

He parked in the graveled lot. Pickup trucks, SUVs and a few sedans filled the lot. Country music blared from the bar, smoke curling outside as they walked up to the door. A few patrons huddled by the fire pit on the rustic planked porch to the side, a gathering spot for smokers and people wanting to escape the loud music inside.

"I know Wanda had addiction problems, but

I can't see her hanging out here," Tia said beneath the beat of the music as they walked to the entrance.

"But it would be a good spot for drug exchanges," Ryder pointed out. "She slips in, orders a drink and leaves with a small package in her purse."

Tia nodded. "I feel for her little boy. I kept hoping she'd get her act together, for his sake."

"Addiction changes people," Ryder said in a gruff voice. "They lose perspective."

"That's true," Tia said softly. Sadness clouded her eyes. "After my folks died, I was prescribed antidepressants, but I didn't like taking them and quickly stopped. I always thought that if I had a child and took care of him, my child would grow up healthy and happy. But…I failed him in the worst way."

Ryder's gut clenched. "This was not your fault, Tia."

He pulled her up against him. Her labored

breathing puffed against his neck as he rubbed one hand up and down her back to soothe her.

"Let's just focus on finding your baby," Ryder said in a low voice. "Hang in there, okay?"

She didn't move for a second, but he felt her relax slightly against him.

He was not going to disappoint her or her baby. Jordie deserved to know his real mother, that she loved him.

The sentiment resurrected the memory of his twin brother's visit. Cash had insisted their mother loved them.

He pinched the bridge of his nose. He didn't want to think or believe that his mother, Myra, had willingly accepted a stolen child.

If she had, she'd lied to him. And if that was true, he didn't know if he could ever forgive that.

TIA BRACED HERSELF for the bar scene. She had to be tough. Not fall apart in Ryder's arms.

It would feel so good if she could lean on him, though.

But leaning on a man wasn't an option.

Especially this man—he had handcuffed her and hauled her to jail.

"You can go back to the car," Ryder said. "I'll handle this."

Tia wasn't a cop or federal agent, but the bar patrons hanging around outside in the parking lot didn't incite a safe feeling. She was surprised there were so many here, too. Judging from the motorcycles, there must be a biker rally nearby.

"This is a seedy-looking crowd," Tia pointed out. "I'd feel better going in with you."

A tense heartbeat passed. For a moment, he looked around, sizing up the situation. When he settled his dark gaze on her, admiration for her mingled with concern in his eyes. "You're right, but keep a low profile. Don't forget that we were shot at earlier."

Tia shivered. "How could I forget?"

Guilt flashed on his face. He didn't have to remind her about their close call. She knew their search was dangerous.

That whoever had taken Jordie didn't want to be found. That he or she would kill to get away.

But she didn't care.

Being close to Ryder Banks was dangerous in another way.

Tia steeled herself against letting her guard down around him, though. He was a tough federal agent. He seemed intent on doing his job.

And he was sexy and strong—just the kind of man a woman wanted to lean on.

She'd seen enough women fall into that trap and come through Crossroads, broken and desperate and in need of help.

She would never forget the lessons she'd learned.

"Just stay beside me," he growled as they went inside.

Tia put on a brave face.

She'd keep her eyes open and her senses alert. Maybe someone in the bar knew who had her son.

Chapter Twelve

Ryder tucked Tia close by his side and visually scoped out the bar as he entered. Protective instincts kicked in, and he looked for male predators, drunks on the watch for a one-night pickup who might target Tia, possible drug dealers or patrons who were high or looking to cut a deal.

Then Wanda.

He didn't know the woman, but this establishment definitely boasted a rough crowd. Booze, conversation, flirting, boot-scooting music and hookups driven by beer and drugs created a chaotic atmosphere. No women with children inside and no couples with an infant.

He kept one hand on Tia's lower back and

guided her toward the bar. Two stools on the end opened up as a couple took to the dance floor, and he led her to it, then sank onto one of the stools.

The bartender, a cowboy with an eye for the ladies, slid two napkins in front of them. “What’ll you have?”

They weren’t here to drink, but he wanted to fit in. “Whatever you have on draft.” He slanted his gaze toward Tia with an eyebrow raise.

“The same.” She plucked a matchbook from the basket on the counter and rotated it between her fingers.

A robust guy wearing a bolo tie approached to her right, his short-cropped hair making his cheeks look puffy. He raked a gaze over Tia, then frowned and walked on past.

“Do you know that guy?” Ryder asked.

Tia studied him as she accepted her beer. “No. Why?”

“Just wondering.” Something about the way the man had looked at Tia raised questions in

Ryder's mind. Had he been simply assessing her to determine if she was single or if she was with him?

Or did he know who she was?

He took a sip of his beer, removed his phone and accessed a picture of Wanda, then laid the phone on the counter. He motioned for the bartender. "Do you know this woman?"

The bartender pulled at his chin as he glanced at it. "Seen her in a couple of times, but I don't really know her."

"Was she with anyone?" Ryder asked.

The bartender wiped the counter with a rag. "Not really."

Ryder had to push. "Was she here to score some drugs?"

The bartender leaned closer, lowering his voice. "Listen, man, I don't know what you've heard, but this is a legitimate place."

"I'm not concerned about the drugs." Ryder eased his credentials from his pocket and discreetly showed them to the man. Then he flicked a finger toward Tia. “This woman’s baby is missing. I’m looking for a lead on the kidnapper.”

Unease darkened the guy’s face. “I don’t know anything about a kidnapping.”

Tia touched the man’s hand, her eyes imploring. “Please think. Wanda may have taken my son. He’s only a few weeks old and he needs me.”

The man gestured for them to wait, took two young women’s orders, gave them their drinks, then returned with the bill.

He slid the check in front of Ryder as if dismissing them. But he’d scribbled a name at the bottom of the bill—Bubba.

“He holes up in an old shack behind the bar,” the bartender murmured.

“He took my baby?” Tia asked.

The guy shook his head. “No, but if anything was going on with Wanda, he’d know.”

Ryder tossed some cash on the bill to pay for their drinks, then shoved back. The big guy who'd been watching Tia stood by the door as they left, his scowl so intense that Ryder hesitated.

But the moment he returned the man's lethal stare, he jammed his beefy hands in the pockets of his jacket and lumbered out the door.

Ryder stepped outside with Tia, his senses alert as he scanned the parking lot. The tip of a cigarette glowed against the dark night. The big guy folded himself inside a jacked-up black pickup, then sped off.

"Who was he?" Tia asked.

"No idea," Ryder replied. "He was watching you inside, though."

Tia shivered. "If Wanda wanted her son back, coming to this bar wasn't the way to do it."

"She made her choices," Ryder said. He just wondered if taking Jordie was one of them. Ryder took Tia's arm again. "The bartender said Bubba lives back here. Let's find that shack."

She fell into step beside him as they wove down the dark alley. The scents of garbage, smoke and urine filled the air, and Ryder led her past a homeless man sleeping in a cardboard box, which he'd propped behind a metal staircase.

Tia paused, her look sympathetic as if she wanted to offer the man assistance, but Ryder ushered her on. Ryder spotted the shack the bartender had referenced, a weathered structure with mud-and-dirt-coated windows.

Not knowing what to expect, he coaxed Tia behind him, removed his gun and held it by his side as he knocked.

A second later, a sound jarred him. Another popping sound, then an explosion.

He grabbed Tia and dragged her away from the building as the glass windows shattered and fire burst through the rotting wooden door.

TIA SCREAMED, DUCKING to avoid flying debris and glass as Ryder pushed her beneath the awning of a neighboring building. He covered her head with his arms and held her, his warmth and strength suffusing her as wood splintered and popped and glass pellets pinged around them.

She heaved for a breath, trembling as they waited for the worst to die down. Finally the force of the explosion settled, but fire blazed behind them, heat searing her.

Ryder breathed against her neck. “You okay?”

She nodded and turned in his arms to face him. He was mere inches away, his gruff expression riddled with anger and worry.

He felt so solid and strong against her, the weight of his body like a wall protecting her. His gaze raked over her face, then dropped to her eyes. A flicker of something masculine darkened his expression, causing a flutter in her belly that had nothing to do with the fact that they could have died in that explosion.

And everything to do with the fact that Ryder was the sexiest man she'd ever laid eyes on.

“What happened?” she asked, her voice cracking with emotion.

His chest rose and fell against hers as he inhaled a deep breath. “Someone warned Bubba we were coming.” Ryder rubbed her arms and lifted his body away from her. “My guess is that he was destroying evidence.”

“It was a meth lab?” Tia guessed.

“That’s what I’m thinking.” He pulled away, retrieved his phone, called for backup and a crime team.

Seconds later, a siren rent the air.

“What if Jordie was in there?” Tia said, panic flaring in her eyes.

“There’s no reason to think that.” Ryder squeezed her arm. “We’ll search the house, but meth dealers generally stick to the drug business.”

Still, fear paralyzed Tia as she looked back at the burning building.

THE NEXT TWO hours passed in a blur of law enforcement officers, rescue workers, firemen and DEA agents. The area was cleared due to fumes from the meth lab, forcing Ryder to get Tia away from the scene.

Thankfully the search indicated that no child or baby had been inside. In fact, no one, adult or otherwise, was inside when the building blew. The theory was that Bubba lit up the place to destroy evidence and any links to himself. Ryder was turning the case over to the DEA.

He had more important work to do.

His phone buzzed as he and Tia drove away from the chaotic scene. "Agent Banks."

"Ryder, we have info on Wanda Hanson," Gwen said. "A cashier at a convenience store called in that she stopped for gas, and confirmed she had a baby with her. No word if it's a boy or girl or the age. But when she left the store, she drove across the street to a motel and checked in for the night."

Ryder's pulse jumped. "Text me the address. I'm on my way."

"What was that about?" Tia asked as he ended the call.

"Wanda Hanson's car was spotted. We're heading there now."

"Did she have Jordie?"

He bit his tongue to keep from offering her false hope. "I don't know. We'll find out."

He pulled to the side of the road, entered the address into the GPS, then swung the SUV around and headed west, toward the highway where the motel was located.

Tia's hands went into motion again, fidgeting and twitching. He laid his hand over hers. Her skin felt cold, clammy. "Try to relax. It's about sixty miles from here."

"What if she's gone by the time we get there?" Fear made her voice warble.

"She checked into a room for the night."

"Hopefully she's feeding Jordie," Tia said.

Ryder wanted to assure her that that was exactly what the woman was doing. But if she was high, drinking or coming down from a high, there was no telling what her mood would be.

Or if she'd even be coherent.

"Did Wanda have a gun?" he asked.

Tia's brows pinched together as if she was thinking. "Not that I recall. Why? Did someone report seeing her with one?"

He shook his head and squeezed her hand again. "No, I was just asking. It's better to be prepared." She could have picked up a gun from a gun shop or borrowed one from a friend.

"When we get there, I need you to remain in the SUV," Ryder said. "I'll go to Wanda's room and see if she's home."

"I'm going, too," Tia whispered. "Jordie needs me."

Ryder shifted back into agent mode. "Let me assess the situation, Tia. We can't go in guns blazing or someone could get hurt." Her. The baby.

"You're right." She released a shaky breath. "If Wanda is doing drugs or drunk, she might panic."

"Right." Half a dozen scenarios of how the situation could go bad flashed through his mind.

He wasn't green at this. Drug addicts and criminals weren't predictable. And when they were backed into a corner, they did things they might never do under normal circumstances.

Tia lapsed into silence. Dark clouds rolled in as the truck ate the miles, the occasional howl of a wild animal breaking the quiet. Traffic thinned, deserted farmland and broken-down shanties a reminder that this highway led out of town and into the vast wilderness.

A good place to hide or get lost. Or disappear with a stolen child.

Ryder sped up and passed a slow moving car, then checked the clock. The minutes rolled into half an hour.

Wanda Hanson was not going to get away tonight, though. Not if she had Jordie Jeffries with her.

TIA GRIPPED THE edge of the seat as Ryder pressed the accelerator and took the curve on two wheels. His calm demeanor was meant to soothe her, but his big body was tense, hands clenching the steering wheel in a white-knuckled grip.

In spite of what he said, he was anxious to get to the motel in case Wanda didn't stay the night.

She fought panic as the time passed.

"Ryder, what if Wanda is meeting someone at the motel? She could be giving Jordie to that person."

Ryder's thick brow rose. "Just try to keep up the faith."

She ran her fingers through her hair, fighting thoughts of the worst-case scenario—that Wanda had disposed of Jordie.

As they neared the motel she noticed a truck pulling an oversize load was parked on the side of the road, a tiny house behind it.

Cheap neon lights glowed ahead, illuminating a graveled parking lot. Ryder veered into the lot and parked between an SUV and a pickup. Two minivans and a sedan were parked at the opposite end, and another vehicle stood in front of the corner unit.

"That's Wanda's van," he said as he killed the engine.

"Do you know which room she's in?" Tia asked.

"Gwen talked to the motel manager. Room twelve, at the end."

Tia zeroed in on the corner unit. A low light burned inside, shrouded by the motel's thin curtains.

Ryder eased his weapon from his holster and reached for the door handle. "Stay here."

Tia nodded, but as Ryder left the SUV and walked toward the minivan, adrenaline and fear made her open her door and follow. Her footsteps crunched on gravel as she hurried up behind Ryder.

He cut her a sharp look. "I told you to wait in the SUV."

Tia peered through the front window of the

minivan, but the windows were tinted, making it difficult to see.

Ryder pulled a small flashlight from his belt and shined it inside, waving it across the front seat. No one there.

He moved to the side window and shined the light across the backseats. Tia's breath caught.

A car seat.

"Look," she whispered. "She has an infant carrier, and there are baby toys."

Ryder gripped her arm. "We have to be careful, Tia. We don't want to spook her. If she has a weapon, this could go south."

Panic seized Tia. If that happened, Wanda might hurt Jordie.

"Trust me," he said on a deep breath.

Ryder's gaze met hers, his dark eyes steady. Determined.

Odd that she did *want* trust him, especially after he'd arrested her. But she did. "You're in charge."

Tension vibrated between them for a long

second. The air stirred around them, bringing the scent of damp earth and garbage. An engine rumbled, doors opened and slammed, and a child's voice echoed in the wind as a family climbed out, gathering toys and suitcases as they walked to their room.

They passed several rooms, then a housekeeping cart. Tia lifted a set of towels from the cart along with a pillow. Ryder nodded in silent agreement and they passed two more rooms, then paused at the last unit.

His right hand covered his weapon, which he held by his side as he knocked with his left.

Tia swallowed hard then called through the door, "Housekeeping. I have extra towels and pillows."

Ryder eased Tia behind him. A voice sounded inside, then footsteps and the door creaked open.

Tia's heart pounded as Wanda appeared. Her eyes were glazed, hair stringy and unwashed, and she reeked of cigarette smoke. As soon as she spotted Tia, she spit out a litany of curse words, then tried to shut the door in their faces.

Ryder shoved the door open, drew his gun and shouted, “Stop and put your hands up!”

Wanda came at him fighting and hissing like a crazy woman, but he yanked both arms down beside her and pushed her against the wall.

Tia spotted a blue bundle lying on the bed between two pillows. Jordie.

She raced toward it.

Chapter Thirteen

Tia ignored Wanda's shrill scream as she approached the bundle on the bed. Ryder wrestled the woman's arms behind her and handcuffed her. She kicked and shouted obscenities as he shoved her into a chair.

Hope speared Tia as she slowly sank onto the bed. She didn't want to startle the baby, so she gently pressed one hand to his back.

Cold fear washed over her. He wasn't moving.

"You can't take my baby!" Wanda shouted.

"Shut up," Ryder growled.

Tia's gaze met his, terror making her heart pound. If Jordie was hurt or sick, she had to help him.

She leaned over and scooped up the bundle, but as she turned him in her arms, shock robbed her breath.

There was no baby.

She was holding a doll in her arms. A life-size doll that felt and looked like a real infant.

But it wasn't Jordie.

"Let me go!" Wanda fought against the restraints so hard that the chair rocked back and forth.

Tia whirled on her. "What did you do with my son?"

Ryder's brows puckered into a frown and he strode over to her to examine the baby. "Good God," he muttered when he realized the truth.

Tia carried the doll over to Wanda. "Where's my baby?"

Wanda shook the chair again as she rocked the chair backward against the wall. "You took my boy away from me. You can't have this one!"

Tia shoved the doll into Ryder's arms, grabbed

Wanda's shoulders and shook her. "What did you do with my son, Wanda?"

"I don't know what you're talking about," Wanda muttered. "You're the one who took my son from me."

Ryder rubbed Tia's back. "Let her go, Tia. She's so strung out she doesn't know what she's doing or saying."

But Tia couldn't let go. She'd been so sure Wanda had her son. So sure he was here, that she'd take him home tonight and feed him and rock him to sleep and wake up in the morning with her family at home.

That this nightmare was over.

"Tell me, Wanda," Tia said in a raw whisper. "Where's Jordie? What did you do with him?"

Wanda went still, her lips curling into a sick smile, yet her eyes weren't focused. They were glazed over with the haze of drugs.

Tia choked on a sob and stepped back, her heart shattering at the realization that Wanda might not have taken Jordie at all.

RYDER GRITTED HIS teeth at the agony on Tia's face. Wanda started another litany of foul words, and he barely resisted smacking her in the mouth.

"Shut up," he barked.

Tia ran a finger over the doll's cheek. The damn thing looked so real he expected it to start crying any minute.

Forcing himself into agent mode, he planted himself in front of Wanda, dropped to a squat and tilted her face to look at him. "Wanda, listen to me. Kidnapping is a felony offense. You need to tell me if you abducted Tia Jeffries's baby."

Her lip quivered as she flattened her mouth into a frown. "Go to hell."

"That's where you're going if you hurt that baby," Ryder said, his tone lethal. "But if you cooperate, I'll see that you get a fair shake, that you receive counseling and treatment for your addiction."

A bitter laugh rumbled from Wanda's throat. "You don't scare me," Wanda said. Her head lolled from side to side as if she was suddenly dizzy or about to crash. "I didn't take that bitch's baby, although it would serve her right if I did, since she ruined my family."

Tia folded her arms and faced Wanda, her body vibrating as if she was grasping to maintain control. "You lost your child because you chose drugs over him."

Ryder pressed a hand to Tia's arm to encourage her to let him handle the situation. "But we can change that," he said, giving Tia a warning look. "Tell me, Wanda. You were hurting because you missed your son. You were angry at Tia. You found out she had a child, and you wanted to get back at her so you—"

"I hope you never get your kid back," Wanda yelled.

Ryder put his arm out to keep Tia from pouncing. Tears flowed from her eyes, ripping at his emotions.

Ryder spoke though gritted teeth. "I told you I'd help you, Wanda, but you have to talk first.

Now, you slipped into Tia's house and you took her newborn—"

"I didn't take the kid." Wanda slid sideways in the chair, her eyes rolling back in her head.

Ryder caught her just before she passed out.

A strangled sob erupted from Tia, her pain and frustration palpable as he phoned 911.

DESPAIR SUCKED AT Tia as the medics rushed in and took Wanda's vitals.

One of the medics gestured toward the doll as they loaded Wanda onto the stretcher. "Is there a child here?" he asked.

Tia shook her head. "She has emotional issues." Whether Wanda's drug addiction or her instability had come first, Tia didn't know.

"She under arrest?" the medic asked.

Ryder cleared his throat. "For now."

"For what?" Tia asked. Being cruel? Traveling with a doll?

"Attacking an officer," Ryder said. "At least

that gives us a reason to hold her until she's coherent."

So he hadn't completely ruled out Wanda as the kidnapper. Although if Wanda had taken Jordie, Tia would have expected her to brag about it, to rub it in her face.

Ryder retrieved Wanda's purse from the desk chair and dumped the contents on the bed as the medics carried Wanda to the ambulance. A baby bottle, wipes, keys, tissues, a pack of gum, a small bag of powder that Tia assumed was cocaine, a tube of dark red lipstick, a pack of matches from the Big Mug, a ratty wallet and a cell phone.

He scrolled through her contacts. "Husband's name is still in here. A few others, but not many. I'll have the lab check them out."

Tia looked over his shoulder. "What about her recent calls?"

A couple of unknowns. The motel number.

The name Horace Laker. A woman named Elvira Mead. The bus station.

Did one of these people know where Jordie was?

RYDER WENT DOWN the list, calling each number. The two unknowns did not respond. Horace Laker was the owner of Laker Car Rentals. Wanda had rented the van from him.

"Did Ms. Hanson have any children with her when you saw her?" Ryder asked.

"Didn't see any. Said she was in a hurry, though. Had to meet up with someone."

Someone who'd taken Jordie, or her dealer?

"Was she high when she talked to you?"

The man coughed. "Didn't think so. But she did seem antsy. But everyone's in a hurry all the time these days so I didn't think much of it."

Ryder thanked him, disconnected, then called the last number. Elvira Mead answered. Ryder introduced himself and explained the situation. "How do you know Wanda?"

"I'm her neighbor," Elvira said. "She called and asked me to feed her cat for a few days. Said she was going out of town."

"Did you see her with a child? An infant, maybe?"

"No, she lost her boy a while back. Thought that might straighten her up, but it sent her into a downward spiral."

"Did she mention a woman named Tia Jeffries?"

"She hated that woman," Elvira said. "Blamed her for her husband leaving her, but we both knew it was Wanda's addiction. He had to take that boy away from Wanda."

Ryder's gut pinched. Hopefully the woman hadn't gotten her hands on Tia's son. "Did she mention getting revenge against Tia?"

A hesitant pause. "She mouthed off some, but if you think she kidnapped that baby, you're wrong. I saw the story on the news. The night the baby went missing, Wanda was passed out at home."

"You're sure about that?"

Elvira gave a sarcastic laugh. "Damn right I am. She barreled in driving like a maniac. Left her car running, crawled out and practically collapsed in the driveway. I went out to check on things, turned off the engine and helped her inside."

"That was nice of you."

A pause. "I've been in AA for twenty years. Kept trying to talk Wanda into joining. I promised her I'd be her sponsor, but she refused to go."

Ryder thanked Elvira for her help and disconnected.

Tia was watching him. "Anything?"

He hated to dash her hopes, but he refused to lie to her. "That was Wanda's neighbor. Wanda was home the night Jordie disappeared—she said she passed out and was there all night."

Ryder checked his watch. It was almost time for the early evening news. "We'll drop her phone off at the crime lab. Gwen can check out her contacts while we go to the TV station."

He hated to put Tia through a public appearance. And it could bring false leads.

But sometimes a parent's grief and fear in a personal plea touched viewers and strangers enough to make them take more interest in helping to find a missing child.

They needed all the help they could get.

TIA FRESHENED UP in the bathroom at the TV station, well aware she looked pale and gaunt. Desperate.

God, she *was* desperate.

The past three days had taken its toll on her body and her mind.

But she had to pull herself together to talk to the press.

On the drive to the station, she'd rehearsed in her mind what she wanted to say. In each scenario, she wound up screaming for the kidnapper to return her baby.

You are not going to fall apart. You're going to be calm, reasonable, tell the truth and...beg.

She tucked her brush in her purse, wiped her face with a wet paper towel, then dried her hands.

Several deep breaths, and she summoned her courage and left the restroom. Ryder was waiting, his gaze deep with concern.

"They're working on Wanda at the hospital," he said. "Gwen just phoned. She didn't find anything suspicious in Wanda's bank records. In fact, Wanda is broke. Probably depleted her money feeding her habit."

"Then she might have been desperate enough to take Jordie and try to sell him," Tia said, her voice laced with horror.

He shrugged in concession. "I'm not ruling out that possibility, although her phone records haven't turned up a lead. And she has an alibi the night of the abduction."

Tia clung to the theory because they had no other clues. "Then she had a partner or help."

Ryder kept his expression neutral. "So far, nothing we've found supports that theory, Tia. According to a neighbor Gwen talked to, Wanda didn't have any friends visiting. She'd alienated all her family. Another neighbor saw a shady-looking character confront her at her car once. She owed him for drugs."

An attractive blonde woman in a dark green dress approached. "I'm Jesse Simpleton. I'll be handling the interview with you, Miss Jeffries."

Tia shook her hand. "Thank you. I appreciate you taking the time to do this."

"Of course." The young woman's voice softened with compassion. "I'm so sorry about your baby. We'll do whatever we can to help."

"I've set up a tip line." Ryder pushed a piece of paper into the woman's hands. "Here's the number."

"We'll make sure it appears on-screen and rebroadcast it with each news segment." Jesse showed them where to sit by the anchor's chair, and the director instructed them regarding the cameras.

Jesse squeezed Tia's hand. "Just talk from the heart."

Tia didn't know what else to do. Before they started, she removed the photo of Jordie she'd taken the night she'd brought him home from her purse and rubbed her finger over her baby's sweet cherub face.

The director signaled it was time to start. Jesse introduced her. Tia angled the photograph toward the camera.

"My name is Tia Jeffries. Six weeks ago was the happiest day of my life. I gave birth to my son, Jordan Timothy Jeffries. He weighed seven pounds, eight ounces and was nineteen inches long." The memory of holding him for the first time made tears well in her eyes. "I carried him home the next morning, ecstatic. He was a good eater and was growing and healthy and happy. But three nights ago, someone slipped in my home while I was sleeping and stole him from his crib." She swallowed, battling a sob.

"I know he's out there somewhere. I can hear him cry at night. I can feel him wanting to come back to me, to be with his mama where he belongs." She pressed a kiss to the photograph. "I don't care who you are or why you took my baby. I don't want revenge or even to see you in jail. All I want is my little boy back." She swallowed hard. "If you have him, please drop him at a church or hospital. No questions asked."

Jesse announced the information about the tip line, but Tia had to say one more thing.

"I'm offering a reward of a hundred thousand dollars to whoever brings him back to me or provides a lead as to where my baby is."

She felt Ryder's look of disapproval, but kept her eyes on the camera as the reward was posted on-screen.

If she had to, she'd use every penny she had to get her son back.

Chapter Fourteen

Tia prayed the TV plea brought in answers, that someone had seen her baby or knew who'd taken him and decided to do the right thing.

Ryder stopped at the diner and insisted she eat dinner, although she could barely taste the food for the fear clogging her throat.

An hour and a half later, he pulled into her driveway, the silence between them thick with tension and the reality that night had come again, another night where she would go into an empty house, with an empty nursery and an empty bed.

"I'll come in and check the house." Ryder slid from the SUV and walked her to the door.

Tia swallowed back emotions as she unlocked the door.

Ryder flipped on a light and strode through the house, checking each room. "The house is clear," he announced as he returned to the kitchen.

She nodded. She hadn't expected the kidnapper to have returned.

Ryder hesitated, his dark gaze penetrating hers as he brushed his fingertips along her arm. She sucked in a breath.

"You did good during the interview, but—"

"If you're going to tell me I shouldn't have offered a reward, don't bother. If the kidnapper took Jordie for money, this should prompt a call. And if not, maybe someone who knows where Jordie is or who took him might step up."

"I just want you to be prepared in case we receive prank calls or false leads."

"I know." Despite the fact that she told herself not to lean into him, she did it anyway. "But we—I—have to do something."

Understanding flickered in his eyes. "You are

doing everything you can," he said. "Trust me. We won't stop until we find your baby."

Tears pricked at her eyes. She needed to hear that, to know that she wasn't alone and that he wouldn't give up. She'd read about cases where leads went cold, other cases landed on their desks and police essentially stopped looking. Children were lost for decades.

Fear nearly choked her. Ryder must have sensed she was close to breaking. He wrapped his arms around her and held her tight.

"Hang in there, Tia."

She battled tears, blinking hard to stem them as she nodded against his chest. His chest felt hard, thick, solid. His arms felt warm and comforting—safe.

His steady breathing and the gentle way he stroked her back soothed her.

But that was temporary. Nothing had changed.

Except that at least she wasn't alone.

She lifted her head to look into his eyes.

"Thank you, Ryder. I'm…glad you're here." She hesitated. "Working the case, I mean."

"I'll let you know if I hear anything." He eased away from her, making her instantly feel bereft and alone again. "Try to get some rest."

She nodded and bit her tongue to keep from begging him to stay.

He walked to the door, shoulders squared, his big body taut with control. "Lock the door behind me," he said as he stepped outside onto the front porch.

She rushed to do as he said, then watched through the window as he climbed in his SUV.

RYDER PINCHED THE bridge of his nose as he drove away from Tia.

He didn't want to leave her, dammit.

But he had no place in her life. Except as an agent working her case.

He checked his phone, but no messages or calls yet. He hoped to hell the TV plea and tip line worked. Or maybe Gwen would locate the woman on that tape at the hospital.

Dark clouds rolled above, thunder rumbling. Most people had tucked their children into bed by now so they'd be safe and sound for the night.

Like Tia had thought her baby was.

Predators were everywhere, though. Watching and stalking innocents. Waiting to strike when the victim let down his or her guard.

By the time he reached his cabin, his thoughts had turned to possibilities other than Tia's ex or Wanda. What if the kidnapping wasn't personal? What if it had nothing to do with revenge against Tia, but simply that she'd crossed paths with a desperate person who wanted a baby, and she'd become the target because she was a single mother?

Images of the agonized look on Tia's face haunted him as he went inside. The rustic place was empty, a chill in the den. He shrugged off his jacket and holster but carried his gun with him, then planted it on the coffee table. The envelope of letters Cash had left was sitting in the center of the table where he'd left them.

He stared at it, struck by the pink rosebuds on the wooden keepsake. His birth mother's doing.

Myra Banks was his mother. She'd rocked him to sleep when he was a baby and nursed his fevers and bandaged his skinned knees and… loved him as much as any mother could.

But this woman… What about her?

Cash insisted he read them, that he understand how much Grace McCullen had wanted the two of them.

He lifted the envelope. Just as Cash said, it was filled with dozens of letters and cards.

He thumbed through them. He didn't know where to start.

Pulse pounding, he walked to the bar in the corner, poured himself a whiskey, then returned. He tossed the first drink back, then poured another and set it on the table.

The picture sitting on the table of him and Myra at Christmas last year mocked him. It had been four years since his father had died. They'd both missed him, although the last few years his father had let his own drinking get out of hand. He'd blamed financial problems, a backstabbing partner who'd cheated him out of half his building supply company.

Even if Ryder and his father hadn't always gotten along and he'd been a bastard to his mother when he was drinking, Myra and Troy had been there for him.

Cash's face, identical to his own, flashed behind his eyes. Cash, his twin, who'd been tossed around in foster care all his life.

Cash, who was now friends—and brothers—with Maddox, Brett and Ray McCullen.

Ryder heaved a sigh. He didn't need a brother. Or to be part of that family.

Still…he had to know the truth.

He dug through the pile, checking the dates, until he found the earliest dated envelope. He opened it and drew out a photograph inside a folded sheet of paper.

He lifted the picture and studied the dark-haired pregnant woman. She was holding a basket of wildflowers. She had her hand on her pregnant belly, and she was smiling up at the sun.

This was the woman who'd given birth to him. She was beautiful.

Emotions flooded him, and he opened the sheet of paper and started to read. Her handwriting was feminine, soft, delicate—her words music to his soul.

Dear son,

This morning, I had an ultrasound and learned I was having twin boys. This is the most exciting day of my life!

I'm not only blessed with one more baby, but two.

As much as the McCullen men need more women around Horseshoe Creek, I honestly believe that God meant for me to have a ranch of boys. The world needs more good men and husbands, and I know you and your brothers will fill that role.

I've already experienced the joy and chaos little boys bring, and also the love and camaraderie they share. I can't wait to add you and your brother to the McCullen clan.

Your father, Joe, is a tough cowboy, but a loving man and father, and you will be blessed by having a role model and leader to guide you through life.

I wish my own mama, your grandmother, could have lived to see this day.

I love you so much my heart is bursting and exploding with emotions. Just a few more weeks, and I'll get to hold you in my arms.

Until then, I'll sing you a lullaby each night while you nestle alongside your twin inside me.

Love always,
Mama

"MAMA LOVES YOU, JORDIE," Tia whispered as she stepped into the nursery. The soothing blues and greens of the room reminded her of the day she'd painted the room in anticipation of her son's arrival.

Ina had knitted baby bootees, and Elle had brought a basket of baby toys. She picked up the blue teddy bear Amy had given her, turned on the musical mobile of toy animals dancing above Jordie's crib and hugged the bear to her as she sank into the chair.

The toy train, football, blocks, arts and crafts corner, puzzles, rocking horse and farm set were all waiting. She rocked the chair back and forth and began to sing "Twinkle, Twinkle Little Star" along with the musical mobile, pushing the chair back and forth with her feet as she cradled the bear to her like she had her son.

For a while, she allowed herself to imagine her little boy playing in the room. She saw him riding the little pony, drawing pictures to hang on the wall, learning to walk, running outside in the backyard and splashing in a rain puddle, then waving to her from the jungle gym at the park.

Of course he'd learn to ride and they'd have picnics and feed the horses and ducks.

A smile tugged at her mouth as she envisioned birthdays and Christmases and marking his growth on the wall chart that she'd hung by the door.

The Hickory Dickory Dock clock on the wall ticked another hour away. Another hour that her son was missing.

ONCE RYDER STARTED with the mail, he couldn't stop himself until he'd read every letter and card. His mother poured out her heart, telling him how much she missed him every day, how she envisioned him and his twin and what they would have looked like, how she put flowers and toys and gifts on their tiny graves, how she quietly celebrated their birthdays.

Then there were disturbing letters where she chronicled her search for the twins. On pink flowered stationery with ink blurred from her tears, she'd written heart-wrenching descriptions of the nightmares that had plagued her. Sleepless nights when she'd wake up sobbing into the pillow because she could hear her babies' cries.

Ryder rubbed a hand over his eyes. God.

Cash was right.

The words on those pages were not from a woman who'd sold her children to fund her and her husband's ranch.

She told about the distance her grief had created between her and Joe, about his affair with Barbara, about how she'd forgiven him because they'd both sought comfort in different ways.

In each progressive letter, she'd promised not to give up looking for them, that she would find them and bring them back to Horseshoe Creek.

The last letter made his heart pound. She'd sensed someone following her. Had felt like she was being watched.

She'd been afraid…

Grief for the woman who'd given birth to him mushroomed in his chest. He traced his finger over her picture, and sorrow brought tears to his eyes.

Next came the face of the woman who'd raised him—Myra Banks.

Dammit. Had she lied about how she'd gotten him, or had the person who'd kidnapped him and Cash lied to her?

He stood and paced. He had to talk to her.

He checked his watch. Ten o'clock.

Dammit, she'd be in bed now.

He'd pay her a visit first thing in the morning. And he'd get to the truth.

TIA DRAGGED HERSELF to the bedroom, forced herself into pajamas and crawled into bed, hugging the teddy bear to her. She sniffed the plush fur, her son's baby scent lingering.

She closed her eyes, but the dark only accentuated the quiet emptiness in the room and in her house.

Her chest ached so badly she could hardly breathe.

Fatigue clawed at her. Just as she was about to drift asleep, her phone trilled.

Tia's pulse jumped.

She swung her legs to the side of the bed and snatched her cell phone. Her hand was trembling so badly she dropped the phone on the floor. Heart racing, she flipped it over.

The caller ID display box showed *Unknown.*

Panic snapped at her nerve endings, but she jerked up the phone and stabbed Connect.

"Hello."

"I saw you on the news."

Tia's breath stalled in her chest. "What? Who is this?"

"Your baby is safe. But he won't be if you keep looking for him."

Terror crawled through Tia. Before she could ask more, the phone went silent.

Chapter Fifteen

Tia trembled as she stared at her phone. The voice had belonged to a woman.

Who the hell was she? Did she really have Jordie?

And what had she meant—he was safe for now? If she kept looking…what would she do to him?

Terror and rage slammed into her. She punched Call Back but it didn't go through.

Tia lurched from bed, strode to the window and peeked out through the blinds. No cars outside. No one in the backyard.

She rushed to the front and looked through the window—no one there, either.

Heart pounding, she pressed Ryder's number. She paced the living room while she waited on him to respond. Three times across the room and he picked up.

"Ryder, I just got a call from a woman who said she has Jordie, that he's safe."

"What?" Ryder said. "Is she bringing him back?"

"No." Tia wiped her forehead with the back of her hand. "She said if I wanted him to stay safe that I should stop looking for him."

Ryder murmured something below his breath. "Dammit, I'm sorry, Tia. I warned you that your interview might draw the crazies and pranks."

"What if it isn't a prank?" Tia cried. "What if she's telling the truth, and we keep looking and she hurts him?" She choked back hysteria. "I'd never forgive myself if something bad happened to him because of me."

RYDER SILENTLY CURSED and walked outside onto the back porch. No way in hell he'd sleep now.

"Listen, Tia, I'll be right over. Meanwhile, I'll call the tech team and see if they can trace that call. Did a name show up?"

"No, it was an unknown."

Of course it was. "Probably a burner. I'll see if anything has come in over the tip line. Stay put and don't panic."

"I'm trying not to," Tia said, her voice cracking with tension. "But I'm scared, Ryder."

"I know." His own gut was churning. If that woman had abducted Jordie, she might be panicking. And if she didn't have him and was just playing some sick, cruel game, she was heartless and deserved to be locked up.

"Hang in there, Tia, I'll be there soon."

Ryder threw a change of clothes and toothbrush in a duffel bag. Then he strapped on his holster and gun, slipped on a jacket, snatched his keys, and headed outside. Out of the corner of his eye, he noticed the mail from his birth mother. He hurried over, stacked everything back inside the envelope and closed it.

The night air hit him, filled with the smell of impending rain.

He jumped in his SUV and sped toward Tia's, calling Gwen as he drove onto the main road.

He explained about the call Tia had received. "I need you to find out where that call came from."

"I'm on it, but if it was as quick a call as it sounds, I doubt we can trace it."

Frustration knotted his shoulders. "I know it, but do your best." They couldn't ignore any call or lead. "Anything from the tip line?"

"Not yet. There have been a few calls, and I have people checking them out."

"What about the woman in the video feed from the hospital nursery? Any ID on her?"

"Afraid not. We're running her through facial recognition and waiting to get the medical records from legal, but so far nothing. I'll keep you posted."

"Thanks." Ryder ended the call, his experience as an agent warring with his worry for Tia and her baby.

You are not supposed to get involved.

But after reading his birth mother's heartfelt words and realizing the pain she'd suffered had only grown deeper with every passing day and hour he and Cash were missing, he realized that Tia was experiencing the same emotions now.

Grace had sensed someone was watching her because she was asking questions about him and Cash.

Tia had just received a threatening call.

Still, he couldn't talk Tia out of giving up her search. Her love—a mother's love—was too strong, just as his birth mother's was.

Only his birth mother's search had gotten her killed.

TIA PACED THE living room, too terrified to sit or lie down. By the time Ryder arrived, she'd worked herself into a sweat.

She yanked open the door and met him on the porch. “Could you trace the call?”

Ryder’s boots pounded the wooden porch floor as he strode toward her. “Gwen’s trying. But most likely it came from a burner phone, Tia. If she calls again and you keep her on the phone long enough, maybe we can get something.”

Tia’s chest tightened. “But what if she doesn’t call again?”

Ryder gripped her arms to stop her constant motion. “We’ll find her another way.”

“But how?” Tia whispered.

Ryder pulled her into his arms and held her. “This is what I do,” he murmured.

She pressed her hand against his chest. His heart beat steadily beneath her palm, soothing her slightly. Ryder was strong and caring and he knew what he was doing.

She had to trust him.

Hard to do when the last man she’d trusted had been Darren, and he’d tried to con her out of her inheritance, then abandoned her when she was pregnant.

He pulled away slightly, then took her hands in his. "When she called, did you hear anything in the background that might indicate where she was?"

Tia strained to remember. "I don't know, I was so terrified..."

"Think. Was there any street noise? Cars? A train? Water?"

"I think I heard a siren."

"Like the police?" Ryder asked.

She shook her head. "No, maybe an ambulance?"

"So she might have been near a hospital," Ryder said.

Tia pressed her fingers to her temple. "Maybe. I don't know, Ryder. It could have been a fire engine."

He squeezed her hands. "Okay, just think about it. Something might come to you later."

Although later might not be soon enough.

RYDER STRUGGLED NOT to show his own anxiety. Tia needed comfort, encouragement and hope.

Lying to her wouldn't be fair.

He insisted that she lie down, but from the couch where he'd stretched out he could hear her tossing and turning.

Just as dawn streaked the sky, she finally settled and fell asleep. She needed rest, so he changed clothes and made coffee, then decided to pay his mother that visit.

By eight o'clock, he'd swung by his place, picked up a couple of Grace's letters and was knocking on Myra's door. She always enjoyed her coffee in the sunroom in the mornings and greeted him with a cup in hand.

"Ryder, what a nice surprise." She wrapped him in a hug. Ryder stiffened slightly. She might not be so happy when he told her the reason for his visit.

Myra pulled back, a small frown creasing her eyes. "Is something wrong, honey?"

Ryder gave himself a second to grasp his emotions before he cleared his throat. "We need to talk. Can I join you in the sunroom for some coffee?"

"Of course." She swept her hand through her wavy chin-length hair and gestured toward the coffeepot. "Do you want some breakfast, too?"

Ryder shook his head. He couldn't eat until this conversation was over.

He chose a mug from her collection, filled it with coffee and they walked to the sunroom together.

She sank into her wicker chair while he took the glider. His father had owned a fifty-acre farm outside town, but when he died, his mother sold it and bought this little bungalow a mile from town. It was a small neighborhood, but catered to retirees who didn't want to deal with yard upkeep.

"What's going on, Ryder?" she asked, tone worried.

"I've been working a case," he said, stalling. "A baby kidnapping."

"Oh, the Jeffries woman. I saw her on the news last night."

He sipped his coffee and gave a nod. "We're hoping the tip line turns up a lead."

"I'm so sorry for her," his mother said. "It must be horrible to have your baby stolen from your home like that."

He studied her but saw no sign of an underlying meaning that she could relate because of him. "She's devastated. She wanted a family more than anything in the world."

Myra traced a finger around the rim of her mug. "Well, I hope you find the baby."

"I will." An awkwardness stretched between them in the silence that ensued. Ryder took another long sip of his coffee. He didn't know where to begin, so he removed a couple of Grace's letters from inside his jacket and laid them on the wrought-iron coffee table.

His mother looked down at them with a frown, then lifted her gaze to meet his. "Talk to me, son. What's going on?"

"It's about my adoption," Ryder said. "I need to know who handled it. How you and Dad got me."

Myra's hand trembled as she lowered her coffee mug to the table. "We've already been through this, Ryder. We wanted a baby and couldn't have one. Your father met this lawyer who said he'd found a little boy for us."

"What was the lawyer's name?"

A seed of panic flared in her eyes before she masked it. "Frost. William Frost."

Ryder made a mental note of the name. "You said he told you that my birth parents needed money, so they sold me in exchange for relinquishing custody."

Frown lines creased her forehead. "Yes."

Ryder had to tread carefully here. This woman loved him and had raised him. He couldn't treat her like a suspect in an interrogation.

But...he had to know the truth. If she'd lied to him or if someone had lied to her...

He gestured toward the envelopes on the table.

"That's not true, Mom," he said gruffly. "I know who my birth parents are now. The McCullens."

His mother gasped. "You talked to them?"

He shook his head. "No, unfortunately they're both dead."

She rubbed her forehead with two fingers. "I don't understand, Ryder."

"They didn't sell me," he said bluntly. "I was kidnapped, stolen from them at birth, along with my twin brother."

Shock and some other emotion resembling guilt streaked her face.

"You knew I had a twin," Ryder said, his throat thickening. "Didn't you?"

Pain and guilt darkened her eyes, then she turned away and wrapped her arms around herself as if she needed to physically hold herself together.

His anger mounted at her silence. "You did, didn't you? You knew about Cash?"

She stiffened her spine. "We were told there were twins, but that one of them was sickly.

And…your father didn't think we could handle a sick child."

"So it wasn't about the money?" Ryder asked.

"Not to the McCullens. And you and Dad lied about paying for me, so you could have taken Cash in, too."

She shook her head, eyes wild with a myriad of emotions. "No, we did pay," she said sharply. "That lawyer wanted a fee, and we used every ounce of our savings to adopt you. We couldn't afford hospital bills for a sick baby and…we thought he'd find a place for your brother."

Rage at the situation fueled Ryder's temper. "But he didn't, Mother." Ryder stood, the glider screeching as it shifted back and forth. He walked to the door and looked out at the woods, needing air.

When he turned back to her, he slammed a curtain down over his face to mask his emotions. "Cash was tossed around from foster home to foster home. He never had a break."

"You met him?" she asked, her voice cracking.

"Yes, he came to see me." The turmoil in Cash's eyes taunted Ryder. "He never had a family, Mother, because you and Dad separated him from me." He pounded his chest with his fist. "And before that, someone kidnapped me and Cash from our birth parents."

Tears blurred her eyes. "I…don't know what to say, son, except that I only knew what the lawyer told us. I raised you. I love you."

Ryder jerked the envelopes from the table and pulled out the photograph of pregnant Grace McCullen, looking up at the sun.

"She was my mother, Cash's mother, and she wanted us. She didn't choose to give us up for adoption."

"That can't be true."

"It is true, Mother. She kept cards and letters she wrote to us. She poured out her heart because she missed us and loved us."

She shook her head in denial. "I'm sorry, Ryder, I had no idea…"

"Maybe not," Ryder said. "But she—her name was Grace—Grace and Joe McCullen not only looked for us, Mother—they died trying to find us."

Chapter Sixteen

Ryder sat in silence as his mother read the first letter. She wiped at tears as she picked up two of the cards and skimmed them.

"My God," she said in a haunted whisper. "I… can't believe this. I…really didn't know, son."

Ryder stood, gripping his coffee mug with clammy fingers. "Maybe not, but you should have told me I had a twin." He faced her, his heart in his throat. "I had other brothers, too, Mother. And parents who grieved that I was taken from them." Just as Tia was grieving.

She jammed the card she was reading back into the envelope. "I'm sorry, Ryder. I don't know what else to say."

He didn't know what else to say, either.

Except the disappointment, sadness and regret for the McCullens—along with his own, for missing out on knowing his brothers—was eating him up inside.

Memories of arguments his mother and father had had when he was a child echoed in his head. His father had been harsh at times, demanding, had always pushed to get his way.

"I know Dad was a tyrant at times, Mother, and that you gave in to him. Do you think he knew the truth?"

She pressed her lips into a thin line. "How dare you disparage your father when he's not here to defend himself, Ryder. He and I both loved you and we did the best we could." She snatched the letters and cards and pushed them into his hands. "There's nothing good to gain by harping on what happened years ago. I've told you the truth, and I'm done talking about this."

Ryder crossed his arms. His mother could be stubborn. She'd always defended his father, even when she knew he was wrong. Now that he was dead, though, he hoped she'd think for herself.

"Fine, then you're right. We're done talking." Furious and confused, he strode back through the house.

Even if his father had known about Cash and the kidnapping, Ryder couldn't confront him. His father was dead.

But…the lawyer might have answers.

His phone buzzed as he sped from the driveway. Gwen.

Hopefully she had news for Tia. He'd also see what Gwen could find out about William Frost.

TIA WOKE TO find Ryder gone. Disappointment mingled with hope that he might be chasing a lead.

Groggy from too little sleep, she showered, scrubbing her hair vigorously to calm her nerves.

Her TV appearance had aired the night before.

Then that call…

But how had the caller gotten her personal cell

phone number? They hadn't released the number on TV.

Surely other reliable calls would come in. Someone who'd seen her baby. Someone who wanted that reward money badly enough to turn the kidnapper in, even if that person was a friend or someone he or she loved.

She checked her phone for missed calls or messages before drying her hair, but there were none.

Outside, she heard a noise. An engine? Car slowing?

She peeked through her bedroom window and scanned the yard. A slight movement. A shadow.

It disappeared as fast as it had come.

Her pulse quickened. Had someone been outside? Was someone watching her or her house?

Or was she simply paranoid?

She blew her hair dry, gathered the strands into a ponytail and brushed her cheeks with powder to camouflage the bags beneath her eyes. Lip gloss helped with her parched dry lips.

She hurried to get coffee and forced herself to eat a piece of toast. The rumbling sound of a car engine startled her, and she rushed to the front window and checked outside.

Ryder.

She swung the door open before he stepped onto the porch. “Gwen just called. It might be nothing or we might have a lead.”

She snatched her purse and phone on the way out the door, then ran back and plucked the baby quilt from the crib just in case they found her son. Pressing it to her chest, she jogged down the steps and crossed to his SUV. “What kind of lead?” she asked as she dived into the passenger seat.

“Someone reported seeing a woman with a baby at the bus station outside Sagebrush acting suspiciously.”

Tia’s breath caught. “Was it a little boy?”

Ryder covered her hand with his. “I don’t know, Tia. It might not be Jordie or the person who kidnapped him. For all we know, the woman is just a nervous traveler, or she could be in trouble for another reason."

"Like an abusive spouse," Tia said, his logic ringing true. Still, she clung to hope as he sped toward Sagebrush.

RYDER TRIED TO banish the image of his mother's pain-filled face from his mind. He had to focus on Tia now.

But…when he had the time, he'd talk to Maddox. As the sheriff of Pistol Whip, Maddox might have information on that lawyer.

Tia twisted her hands together. "Who called about the woman?"

"A ticket salesperson at the bus station."

"Did she get a look at Jordie?"

"She didn't say." He didn't want to squash the light in Tia's tone, but he also didn't want to feed false hope.

Tia chewed on her bottom lip, then lifted the baby blanket and pressed it against her cheek.

Early morning sunlight slanted off her face, making her skin look golden and her face young.

He thought of his birth mother, Grace, in the picture where she was her pregnant. She'd looked radiant and happy, just as he imagined Tia had during her pregnancy.

He wished he could have seen Tia like that, before the horror and agony of this kidnapping had taken its toll.

She remained quiet as he maneuvered through town.

Just as they pulled up, a bus was loading, a line of passengers boarding. Tia leaned forward to search the group as he swung into a parking space. Before he killed the engine, she threw the door open and started toward the bus.

But the bus door quickly closed, the engine fired up and the bus pulled away.

Tia cried out in frustration.

Dammit. Ryder motioned to the entrance of the station and darted inside. He strode straight to the ticket counter, flashed his ID and explained he needed to speak to the person who'd phoned the tip line.

A white-haired woman in a green shirt emerged from the back. "I'm Bernice, the lady who called."

Tia rushed up behind him, her breathing choppy. "This is my son, Jordie." She shoved the photograph toward Bernice. "Did the woman you saw have this baby with her?"

Ryder placed a hand to her back as they waited on a response.

TIA'S HEART WAS pounding so hard she thought it would explode in her chest.

Bernice leaned over the counter and scrutinized the photograph. "Hmm, I can't be sure. She had him wrapped up tight in a baby blanket and kept him to her chest, so I couldn't see the baby's face."

Tia gripped the counter. "Did you see the baby's hair? Was it blond or dark?"

Bernice settled her reading glasses on the end of her nose. "I…I'm sorry, I can't say."

Ryder gave Tia's waist a squeeze, a silent message to hang in there.

"Why did you think she was acting suspiciously?" Ryder asked.

Bernice worried her glasses with her fingers, settling and resettling them again. "Well…she was awkward, you know, like she didn't know how to take care of the baby. It was fussing and crying and she jostled it to try to quiet the poor thing and kept looking around as if she was afraid."

Because she had Jordie?

Or had Ryder been right—was she running from someone else? God knew, Tia had worked with enough women coming through Crossroads that that was a distinct possibility.

"Did she call the baby by name?" Ryder asked.

Bernice glanced at the other ticket attendant, but the heavyset woman simply shrugged. "I was on my break, didn't see or hear nothing."

"A name?" Ryder asked again.

Bernice shook her head no. "She just kept saying, 'Hush, little darlin'.' That's all."

"What was the passenger's name?" Ryder asked.

Bernice checked the computer. "Vicki Smith."

"Did you check her ID?" Ryder asked.

The woman nodded. "All she had with her was a discount store card, one of those big warehouse deals where you have to have a membership."

"No driver's license?" Tia asked.

She shook her head no. "Said her wallet was stolen. Sounded down on her luck."

"What's her destination?" Ryder asked.

Bernice glanced at the computer again. "Cheyenne."

"Can you give me a description of her?"

"She was wearing a scarf, so I don't know how long her hair was, but it was a dirty brown."

"Height and weight?"

Bernice shrugged. "About your height, ma'am. But she was plumper, although hard to tell how plump with the baby pressed to her like that. Could have been baby weight, too."

"Did she have any distinguishing marks on her body? A tattoo or birthmark?"

"Not that I saw," Bernice replied.

"Did she mention meeting anyone?"

"No."

"Did she make any calls? Maybe on a cell phone?"

Bernice hesitated again then shook her head. "I didn't see a phone. Like I said, though, she was acting strange, like she didn't want to talk to people. So I didn't push it."

Ryder thanked her, then pressed a card on the counter. "If you think of anything else she said or did, call me."

Tia clutched the baby blanket to her as she followed Ryder back to the SUV. "What are we going to do?"

Ryder started the engine, a muscle ticking in his jaw. "We're going to follow that bus."

He gunned the engine and sped onto the highway. Tia buckled up for the ride.

RYDER HONKED HIS horn as a sedan nearly cut him off when he pulled out of the bus station. The black car ignored the horn, sideswiped him then raced on.

Ryder swerved, hit the curb and bounced back onto the road. He wanted to go after the son of a bitch, but following that bus and the woman on board took priority.

Tia's breathing filled the strained silence. She gripped the dashboard and said nothing, though.

Instead she kept her gaze trained ahead, eyes darting back and forth in search of the bus.

Ryder spotted it ahead, flew around an ancient pickup and roared up beside it.

"Look!" Tia pointed to a side window near the back, where a young woman wearing a dark scarf turned to watch them.

Dammit, she had a baby on her shoulder,

swaddled in a blanket, and her eyes were wide with fear.

"That has to be her," Tia said in a raw whisper.

Chapter Seventeen

Ryder considered pulling the bus over, but decided to wait until the next bus station. It was only twenty minutes away.

Meanwhile, he phoned Gwen and asked her to dig up what she could find on Vicki Smith.

"I'm following the bus she's on now," Ryder said. "She used a discount store's ID, no driver's license, so it may be a fake name."

"Smith is an extremely common name," Gwen said. "Let me see how many Vickis there are."

A traffic light turned yellow, but the bus coasted on through just as it turned red. Tia looked panicked. Ryder quickly checked the intersection for cars, then sped through.

No way were they going to lose this bus.

"Ryder, I found dozens of women named Vicki Smith, but none match the description you gave, either. But if this woman is the unsub, she could have changed her appearance."

"I know. Cross-check with those medical records we got warrants for and see if any of those women recently delivered a baby or lost a child."

"On it."

The bus slowed at another light. The woman turned around again, fear flashing on her face when she realized they were still behind her.

"Okay, a woman named Vicki Smith gave birth to a baby girl a month ago in Sagebrush."

"Find out where she is now and the status of the baby."

"Okay, I'll keep you posted."

She disconnected just as the bus moved forward. It swung a wide left at the intersection and Ryder followed it into the parking lot of the bus station.

TIA DARTED AROUND the front of the bus just as the door opened and passengers began to unload.

Ryder rushed up behind her. “Stay calm and let me handle the situation,” he said in a low voice next to her ear.

Tia felt anything but calm. She rose on tiptoes to see over the passengers, desperate to find the woman and baby. The bus was full, though, and the woman had been sitting near the back, so she couldn’t do anything but wait.

“What did you learn about her?” Tia asked as an Asian woman and small child walked past her, followed by two teenagers, earbuds in, immersed in their music.

“Nothing, really. A woman named Vicki Smith gave birth to a baby girl a month ago. Gwen’s looking into her.”

Several more passengers left the bus, then the bus driver peered to the back of the bus, seemed to decide that was everyone getting off at this stop and closed the door.

"No!" Tia hit the door with her palm.

Ryder stepped in front of her and rapped his fist on the door, then flashed his badge at the window. "FBI, open up."

The bus driver flicked a hand up, indicating he was going to comply, then opened the door. Tia started to board, but Ryder gently urged her to stay still.

"Let me handle it, Tia." He flashed his badge as he climbed the steps. Tia followed on his heels.

Whispers and murmurs passed through the remaining passengers still seated.

"FBI Special Agent Ryder Banks," Ryder announced.

Tia scanned the people on board and spotted the woman in the back huddling down in the seat, her head buried against the baby. A scarf covered her hair, shadowing her face.

Ryder held up his hand. "Please stay seated, folks. I need to talk to the young woman in the back, the one with the baby."

The woman remained crouched in the seat, face averted as she soothed the crying child.

Tia's heart ached. Was that Jordie crying for her?

Ryder motioned for the woman to come with him. She stood slowly, hugging the baby to her as she followed Ryder.

"This should just take a moment," he said to the woman and the bus driver.

Tia shaded her eyes from the sun as she exited the bus into the parking lot. Ryder guided the woman to the sidewalk.

The woman pivoted, covering the baby with her hand to hide its face.

"Miss," Ryder said, "what is your name?"

She cast a terrified look at Tia then patted the bundle in her arms. "Vicki Smith."

"And your baby's name?"

"Mark," the woman said. "Why? What do you want with us?"

Tia cleared her throat. "Do you know who I am?"

Vicki adjusted her scarf, drawing it tighter. “No. Should I?”

Tia barely restrained herself from yanking the child from the woman’s arms. “I was on the news last night. My baby was kidnapped I’ve been looking for him ever since.”

The woman backed away. “I don’t have your baby. This is my child. I’m going to visit my mother in Cheyenne.”

Ryder gently touched the baby’s cap. “Then we can clear this up really quickly. Just let us see the baby.”

She shook her head vigorously, clutching the child as if to protect it from them. “You can’t take my baby. I won’t let you.”

Tia inhaled sharply. The fear in the woman’s voice was real. Whether it was because she was a kidnapper or for another reason, she couldn’t tell.

Ryder gently touched the baby again. “I’m not going to take the child. But I need to verify that this is not Miss Jeffries’s son.”

"It's not," the woman cried. "Now let me go. If I miss that bus, I can't get to my mother's."

"Just show me that it's not my son," Tia said, softening her tone. "Then we'll let you be on your way."

The woman trembled, her eyes wary as she studied them. But she slowly tilted the infant back into her arms and eased the blanket from its face.

Ryder gently pushed the cap back to reveal a thick head of wavy black hair.

It wasn't Jordie.

TIA'S LEGS BUCKLED. Ryder steadied her, sensing her disappointment.

"I'm sorry, you're right," Tia said. "I just thought…"

"Someone phoned the tip line and said you were acting suspiciously," Ryder said, still unwilling to release her before he heard the real story.

She *was* acting suspiciously and hiding something.

Alarm speared the woman's eyes. "I...don't know what you mean." She hurriedly rewrapped the infant and started back toward the bus.

Ryder caught her arm. "Wait, I need to ask you some questions."

Vicki's eyes darted around the parking lot. "Please, you can see I don't have that woman's child. Now let me and my baby go."

"Something's wrong," Ryder said. "Is that child really yours?"

"Of course it is," she gasped.

"Then why the fake ID? Because I know Vicki Smith is a fake name."

"No, I'm Vicki. I'm from Pistol Whip—"

"There is a Vicki Smith from Pistol Whip, but she gave birth to a baby girl a month ago."

The woman sagged against his hold. "Please don't do this. If he finds us, he'll kill me and take Mark. He's already hurt him once. I won't let him do it again."

Tia had eased up beside him. “I’m sorry for scaring you, Vicki.”

“Are you talking about your husband or boyfriend?” Ryder asked.

Embarrassment heated the woman’s cheeks. “Yes.”

“He’s Mark’s father?”

“Yes—”

“How did he hurt him?” Ryder asked.

The woman rocked the baby. “He can’t stand it when he cries. He shakes him so bad. And the other night he threw him against the wall.”

Pure rage shot through Ryder. If she was telling the truth, the bastard should be locked away.

“The real Vicki and I are friends,” she continued. “She loaned me her discount card so I could use it as an ID to get on that bus.”

“Is your mother really waiting?” Tia asked.

The woman shifted, then shook her head, fear and defeat streaking her face. “No… I have no place to go, but I had to get away from him.” She dropped a kiss on the baby’s head. “I put up with him hurting me, but I refuse to let him beat up our son."

"Good for you," Tia said with a mountain of compassion in her voice.

"I'm sorry about your situation," Ryder said injecting sympathy into his voice. "But if what you're saying is true, you should go through the proper channels."

"I filed a police report once, and they came and talked to him." Her voice grew hot with anger. "Then do you know what he did?"

"He was enraged and took it out on you," Tia said.

"Yes," the woman whispered brokenly. "He beat me so bad I couldn't walk for days. Where were the police then?"

Ryder silently cursed. He'd heard this story before, too.

"I can help you," Tia said. "I run a program called Crossroads. It's for families in crisis. There are other women like you, women who will help you."

"But he'll find me," Vicki cried. "He always finds me."

"No," Tia said emphatically. "I promise you he won't."

"She's right," Ryder said. "If everything you're telling me is true, I'll make certain you and your child have protection."

The woman began to sob, and Tia drew her and Mark into a hug, comforting them while Ryder motioned to the driver that he could leave.

TIA'S HEART ACHED for the woman. Unfortunately her story was a common one. The cycle of abuse would repeat itself if she didn't break it. That took strength and courage and help from strangers.

She could offer that. And if Ryder was willing to help...

The woman's body trembled next to Tia as she helped her into the SUV. She wished they had a car seat for the infant. They would take care of that ASAP.

Ryder phoned a friend with a private security company, and he agreed to guard the center for the evening. She phoned Elle to give her a heads-up about the situation. Vicki admitted her real name was Kelly Ripples.

Tia hugged Kelly again as they arrived at the center. "Everything will be okay now, I promise."

Elle and Ina met them at the door. "We fixed a room for you and the baby," Ina said. "I hope you don't mind sharing a room. Susan and her little girl are really nice. They just got here a couple of days ago. I think you'll like them. The little girl loves babies."

Kelly looked skeptical, but thanked Ina and followed her to one of the bedrooms, where a portable crib was set up in the corner. "I need to feed him," Kelly said.

"Of course," Tia said. "We'll let you have some privacy."

Ina gestured toward the rocking chair. "When he's settled, please join us in the dining room. I cooked a pot of homemade vegetable soup and some corn bread."

"That sounds wonderful," Kelly said in a low voice.

Tia joined Ryder in the hallway. "Thank you for arranging for the security guard."

He nodded. "I called Gwen. She's checking Kelly's story."

"I believe her," Tia said.

Ryder crossed his arms. "Time will tell. Until then, she'll be safe here. And if her story is confirmed, I'll see that her husband never gets hold of that child again."

Tia had never trusted a man the way she did Ryder. His fierce protectiveness and drive for justice was admirable.

She wanted to tell him that, but her growing feelings for him terrified her.

THE COMPASSION TIA showed for the woman astounded Ryder. She had gone from suspecting

Kelly of kidnapping to an offer to help her in minutes.

Ryder's cell phone buzzed. He motioned to Tia that he needed to take it, so he stepped into the other room. "Gwen, that was fast."

"It's not about Kelly," she said quickly. "We have a hit on the woman in the security footage at the hospital nursery, and I cross-checked it with the hospital records. Her name is Bonnie Cone. She lives outside Sagebrush. She lost a baby recently and suffered serious depression. Her husband claimed she was obsessed with having another baby right away, but the doctor advised against it. The husband said they separated last month. He hasn't been able to reach her for a couple of weeks and he's worried."

A desperate, grieving woman. "Where is she?"

"I'm texting you her address now."

Ryder considered pursuing the lead on his own, but if they found Bonnie Cone, Tia could tell them really quickly if she had Jordie.

Chapter Eighteen

Tia assured Kelly that she and Mark would be safe at Crossroads. The private security agent seemed to take his job seriously.

His eyes also lit up with a spark when he met Elle.

Tia would love to see her friend with a nice man. She'd had her own troubles before joining Crossroads and deserved happiness. But she definitely had built walls to protect herself.

Just as Tia had done.

Maybe that was the reason they were such good friends.

Ryder explained the phone call, and they

rushed toward Sagebrush. She fidgeted, determined not to get her hopes up.

"The woman we're going to see was the one on the security camera at the hospital. Her name is Bonnie Cone. She lost a baby over a month ago. According to Bonnie's husband, she was despondent and obsessed with having another child."

Tia's heart went out to her.

But…her sympathy would only stretch so far.

The afternoon sunlight beamed in the car and slanted off farmland as they passed. Beautiful green grass, cows grazing, horses galloping on a hill in the horizon—a reminder of Wyoming's natural beauty. Normally those things soothed her, but today nothing could erase the grave feeling in her chest.

Bonnie's house was an older ranch, set off the road in a neighborhood about five miles from town. Although the house had probably been built fifty years ago, it looked reasonably well kept, except for the yard.

A gray minivan was parked in the drive. As they passed it, she peeked in and spotted a car seat.

They walked to the front door in silence. A welcome home wreath on the door and a wooden bench on the front stoop indicated that Bonnie had tried to make the house more homey and inviting.

Ryder punched the doorbell, his gaze scanning the property. He was always on alert. A product of his job, she supposed.

How did he live this kind of life, facing danger and criminals every day, and not become jaded? Did he ever relax?

He punched the bell a second time and Tia peeked through the front window. Living room with a brown sectional sofa, magazines dotting the coffee table, along with a baby bottle and an assortment of infant toys. A colorful blanket was spread on the floor, a toy rabbit and squeaky toy on top.

Seconds later, footsteps sounded and she

quickly moved away from the window. If the woman saw her, she might bolt.

RYDER FLASHED HIS ID as Bonnie opened the door. “Miss Cone, my name is Special Agent Ryder Banks, and this is Tia Jeffries.”

Bonnie’s gaze darted to Tia, her eyes widening in recognition. “You’re the woman on TV last night.”

“Yes, that was me,” Tia said softly. “Can we come in?”

Bonnie glanced back and forth between Tia and Ryder. “I don’t understand.”

Bonnie looked pale and thin, her eyes were dark with circles, her medium brown hair curly and tousled as if she hadn’t slept in days. She was also still wearing a bathrobe.

Ryder shouldered his way through the door. “We need to talk. It’ll just take a moment.”

Bonnie tugged the belt of her robe tighter around her waist and gestured toward the sofa.

Baby clothes and crib sheets overflowed a laundry basket, spilling onto the sofa.

Tia exhaled and slid the basket to the floor so she could seat herself beside Bonnie. Ryder claimed the club chair opposite her.

Bonnie plucked a receiving blanket from the basket and wadded it in her hands. “What is this about?”

“We’re investigating the disappearance of Miss Jeffries’s baby,” Ryder said.

“I’m sorry about your son.” The woman gave Tia a sympathetic smile. “But what does that have to do with me?”

“You delivered your baby at the same hospital where I gave birth,” Tia said.

Pain darkened Bonnie’s eyes. “Yes.”

“I know you lost a child,” Tia said gently. “That must have been awful.”

Bonnie’s lower lip quivered. “It was.”

“I’m so sorry,” Tia said. “I understand the heartache.”

“No one understands,” Bonnie said with a

trace of bitterness. "I carried him for nine long months inside me. I had dreams for him."

Tia placed her hand over Bonnie's. "I do know. I carried my baby just like you did, I dreamed about holding him and watching him grow up. I started a college fund for him before he was even born."

Ryder swallowed hard at the emotions her words stirred.

"We were watching the video feed from the hospital," Ryder cut in. "You were on it."

Bonnie narrowed her eyes. "What?"

"After your baby was gone, you came back to the hospital and you were looking at the newborns."

Bonnie made a strangled sound in her throat and placed her hand over her stomach. "Yes, I wanted a baby so badly. I missed my son."

"That's understandable," Ryder said. "You missed him so much that you were out of your mind with grief."

Bonnie nodded, tears welling in her eyes.

She swiped at them, unknotted the blanket and began to fold it methodically, as if the task was calming.

Tia picked up a burp cloth from the basket and ran her fingers over it. "We know you were grief stricken and in a bad place, Bonnie. I understand that, I do."

"Maybe you were so distraught you did something you never would have done otherwise," Ryder said. "You wanted to replace your baby, so you found another one."

Bonnie's startled gaze shot to Ryder's. "Yes, I did. My husband didn't understand, but I had to have a baby." Her voice was raw, agonized. "What's wrong with that?"

"Nothing," Tia said. "Not unless you took my son to replace yours."

Bonnie stood abruptly, knocking the basket of laundry over. Clothes spilled out, but she didn't seem to notice. "My God, that's the reason you're here. You think I kidnapped your baby?"

Ryder stood, sensing the woman might turn volatile. “We have to ask.”

Bonnie fisted her hand by her side. “That’s completely insane,” Bonnie stuttered. “I would never do such a thing.”

A mixture of emotions welled in Tia’s eyes. Ryder wanted to comfort her, but she needed answers instead.

“But you got another baby,” Ryder asked.

Fear deepened the panic in Bonnie’s expression. “Yes, but that baby is mine now.” She whirled toward Tia. “He’s not yours, do you hear me? He’s mine and you can’t take him away.”

Tia pressed a hand to her mouth.

“Then where did the baby come from?” Ryder asked.

“I didn’t steal anyone’s baby,” Bonnie shouted. “I adopted a little boy.”

Tia’s sharp breath rent the air. “Then you won’t mind showing him to me.”

Anger slashed Bonnie’s expression. “If it’ll get

you to go away and leave me alone, then yes. I'll get him."

She stalked toward the bedroom, and Tia and Ryder followed. For all he knew, she was going to grab the baby, go out a back door and run.

TIA RUSHED TO stay close to Bonnie in case she snatched the baby and tried to get away.

Bonnie stumbled, then grabbed the bedpost to steady herself as she crossed to the bassinet.

"He's sleeping," she said in a voice both tender and filled with fear. "I hate to disturb him."

Tia and Ryder remained in place, though, so she gently lifted the infant, swaddled in a blue blanket with turtles on it, his tiny fingers poking out.

Tia's pulse pounded as Bonnie gently pulled the blanket back to reveal the baby's face.

He had a fuzzy blanket of brown hair, his chin was slightly pointed, his face square. He was beautiful.

But he wasn't Jordie.

Disappointment nearly brought her to her knees.

Tia grabbed the bedpost this time, choking back a cry.

"Tia?" Ryder's low, gruff voice echoed behind her.

She shook her head, then turned to face him, her heart in her eyes.

Ryder crossed the room and took her arm, then glanced at the baby.

"How old is he?" Ryder asked.

"Four weeks today." Bonnie dropped a kiss on the baby's head, making Tia's heart yearn for Jordie even more. "Isn't he beautiful?" Bonnie said in a voice reserved for doting mothers.

"Yes," Ryder said. "You said you adopted him?"

"I did. After I lost…my child, I was devastated. Then my doctor advised against another pregnancy and I thought I couldn't go on." She paused and swiped at tears. "One of the counselors suggested adoption. I thought it would take a while, but someone else in the hospital gave me the name of a lawyer who handled private adoptions, and I contacted him." She rocked the infant back and forth in her arms. "It was a miracle. He said he knew of a teenager who had decided to go the adoption route. I couldn't believe it." She hugged the infant tighter. "As soon as she gave birth, he called me. I rushed to the hospital and there he was in the nursery, all wrapped up, just needing some love."

Her eyes brightened. "Love I could give him. I knew he was meant to be mine. I needed him and he needed me."

"He's lucky to have you," Tia said.

Bonnie nodded. "I named him after my father, David. He was a good man."

"It's a lovely name," Tia said. "I'm sure your father would be happy."

"What was the lawyer's name?" Ryder asked.

"He's a reputable attorney," Bonnie said defensively.

Ryder arched a brow. “His name?”

“Why do you want to know?” She clutched the baby tighter. “Did you talk to my husband? If you did, he probably told you I was crazy, that I was obsessed with having another child. And I was, but that doesn’t mean I won’t be a good mother to this little guy.”

“I’m not questioning that,” Ryder said. “But I’d like to talk to the lawyer just in case whoever abducted Tia’s baby might have done so to sell him.”

“Sell him?” Bonnie gasped. “My God. It’s not like I bought him off a black market. What kind of person do you think I am?”

“It’s no reflection on you, Bonnie,” Ryder said. “But in a missing child case, I have to consider every possible theory.”

Tia wanted to reassure her everything would be all right. But if, by chance, she had adopted a child obtained illegally, that adoption would be illegal and the courts would intervene.

That scary realization must have occurred to Bonnie.

"You can't take him," Bonnie said. "I can't lose him, too."

Tia stepped closer to calm her. "We're not going to do that, Bonnie. We just need the name of that lawyer."

Her expression wilted, and she closed her eyes for a second as if in a silent debate. When she opened them, she clenched her jaw. "His name is Frank Frost. His office is in Cheyenne."

"Frost," Tia said. "Thank you, Bonnie. We'll let you go and rest." She stroked the back of the baby's head. "You sleep tight, sweetie. Bonnie loves you and will take good care of you."

Ryder glanced at Tia. "Let's go."

Anxiety tightened her shoulders as she followed him outside. "Ryder, what's wrong?"

"I don't know," Ryder said as he climbed in the front seat.

A muscle ticked in his jaw as they pulled away.

"Are you keeping something from me?" Tia asked.

Emotions glittered in Ryder's eyes, but he quickly masked them. "No."

"Yes, you are," Tia said earnestly. "You promised not to lie to me, Ryder. If you heard something about Jordie—"

"I didn't," he said, his wide jaw hard with anger. "But I recognize that name Frost."

Tia pulled the baby quilt into her lap and twisted her hands in the soft fabric. "What about him?"

Ryder heaved a weary breath. "I was adopted myself. I've always known it, but recently I learned who my birth family was—is. I have a twin brother, Tia. We were kidnapped as babies and our parents were told we were dead."

A cold chill swept over Tia. "You were kidnapped?"

He nodded. "My twin brother has reconnected with our birth family. He came to see me the other day."

“Oh, my God.” Tia laid a hand on his shoulder, aching to comfort him for a change. “That must have been a shock.”

“It was.” He hesitated, then cleared his throat. “The lawyer who handled my adoption was named Frost.”

Tia froze. “You think it was the same man?”

“No, his name was William. But they could be related.”

“Are you suggesting the lawyer knew that you and your brother were stolen?”

Ryder shrugged, but his look indicated he did.

Chapter Nineteen

Another thought occurred to Ryder as he drove toward Cheyenne.

If Frost had intentionally been an accomplice in the kidnapping and selling of babies—him and Cash—was that the first instance?

How many more had there been since?

He'd have to talk to the McCullens—see if they'd looked into the lawyer. But the thought of meeting his brothers made his gut clench.

He wasn't ready for that. Not with the memory of those letters fresh in his mind.

Worse, now he'd divulged his secrets to Tia. She'd grown silent, obviously contemplating the implications of his statement.

He spotted a barbecue restaurant and pulled into it. "Let's get a quick lunch. I need to call Gwen."

Tia nodded, worry radiating from her features as they made their way inside. They grabbed a booth and ordered, then he stepped outside to phone Gwen.

"I checked into Kelly Ripples's story," Gwen said. "She's telling the truth. She's been in the hospital three times over the past year with injuries consistent with spousal abuse. A neighbor reported a domestic at her place six weeks ago. Found a pregnant Kelly on the floor bloody and bruised."

"Son of a bitch."

"Yeah, he's a bad one. Good for her for getting away from him."

"We just have to keep him away," Ryder said. It was a damn shame women needed help to escape the men who supposedly loved them. But better for the child to not have a father than have one who hit him.

"I have someone else I want you to run a background check on. A lawyer named Frank Frost. He has a practice in Cheyenne. Also look for info on William Frost."

"What are you looking for?"

Ryder explained his personal situation, including the history behind his own adoption, brushing over Gwen's murmur of sympathy. "The woman in the video, Bonnie Cone, used Frank Frost for legal services in a recent adoption. I need to know if that was legitimate, if adoptions are his specialty, if there have been any complaints against him—"

"I got it. I'll get back to you ASAP."

He thanked her, then hung up and started inside. A breeze blew in, stirring dust. A ranch in the distance reminded him of the McCullens and Horseshoe Creek.

He had to put aside his feelings and talk to the McCullens. See if they had insight on either of the Frost men. If Maddox had investigated him, it could save Ryder time.

Stomach knotted, he punched Cash's number.

"Ryder?"

"Yeah," Ryder said. "I read the letters."

A tense moment stretched between them. "They wanted us."

"I know that now."

"You want to come by Horseshoe Creek and talk?"

Did he? "Sometime. But I'm mired in this kidnapping case right now. Actually, that's the reason I called."

"What do you need?"

An odd feeling tightened his chest. He'd always worked alone. Been a loner all his life.

Now he had brothers.

Cash had offered to help, no questions asked.

"I need to know if you or any of the McCullens know anything about a lawyer named William Frost."

A heartbeat passed. "Frost?"

"Yeah. He's the lawyer who handled my adoption. I wondered if he was in on our kidnapping."

Cash's breathing echoed over the line. "I'll talk to Maddox and Ray and call you back."

Ryder thanked him and disconnected. He had to get back to Tia. She was anxious for news.

He wished to hell he had some.

TIA TRIED TO eat her pulled pork sandwich, but she could barely swallow the food. Her stomach was churning.

Ryder had been kidnapped as a baby. Her son had also.

And now that Ryder knew the truth, it was too late for him and his birth parents to reconcile.

What if that happened to her and Jordie? Was she doomed to a life where she searched the crowd everywhere she went, hoping to see a child that was her son? As the years went on and he changed, would she even recognize him?

She sipped her tea to wash down the sandwich. "I've been thinking." She set her tea glass on the table. "If this lawyer is involved in something illegal, he's not going to just come out and tell us."

Ryder's jaw tightened. "No. I'll need a warrant for his records."

"That's not easy," Tia said. "Not with adoption or medical records."

"Gwen's seeing what she can dig up, and I called Cash to see if the McCullens know anything about Frost. They're both going to get back to me."

He dug into his sandwich, and Tia toyed with an idea in her head. "You're planning to talk to Frank Frost?"

Ryder nodded as he chewed. "I'm hoping to find out something to use as leverage to persuade him to talk."

"I have an idea." Tia tapped her nails on the table. "Why don't we pose as a couple wanting to adopt a baby?"

Ryder scrubbed a hand through his hair. "That's not a bad idea, Tia, but you were on TV. He'll recognize you."

Tia's pulse jumped. She hadn't thought of that. "Wait a minute," she said, her mind spinning. "I'll wear a disguise."

He took another bite of his sandwich and wiped his mouth with the gingham napkin. "I don't know. He might see through it."

Tia's mouth twitched. "Trust me, Ryder. I've done this before." At his perplexed look, she continued, "I mean, for other women."

Ryder studied her as he finished his meal. "I don't need to know details," he said.

Because he sensed what she'd done might have crossed the lines with the law. It had a few times. But sometimes the law failed.

"All right. But I think it could work."

Ryder ordered a cup of coffee and pie. "It's worth a shot, although if he recognizes you and realizes what we're doing, it could be dangerous."

"I don't care," Tia said. "I don't want Jordie to be lost to me forever like you were to your parents."

Her comment hit home and brought pain to his eyes.

"I'm sorry. I—"

"You're just speaking the truth," Ryder said. "I admire that, Tia. I've been lied to enough in my life."

Tia laid her hand over his and stroked it. "What do you mean?"

He glanced at their hands, and she expected him to pull away. But he didn't. He turned his hand over beneath hers and curled his big fingers around hers.

"My father is dead, but I talked to my mom. She claims she didn't know I was kidnapped, but she and Dad knew I was a twin. They didn't take my brother because he was sickly." His tone turned gravelly with anguish. "Cash was never adopted. He bounced from one foster home to another and had a rough life."

Tia had heard similar stories.

"That's sad," Tia said. "Is he all right now?"

Ryder nodded, his frown softening. "He's connected with the McCullens and is married. He even adopted two kids."

Tia rubbed his palm. "That's a great ending to the story. He used what happened to make him stronger and to give back to needy children."

"But he could have grown up with me, had a decent upbringing—"

"You feel guilty that you got the better deal," Tia said, sensing guilt beneath the surface of his words.

His troubled gaze lifted to hers, and he gave a quick nod.

"It's not your fault," Tia rushed to assure him. "You were an innocent kid, a baby when you were taken. You didn't know about him."

"Not until this week." Resentment deepened his tone.

Tia's heart ached for him. "You're angry at your mother because she didn't tell you about him."

He nodded again. "How could she keep that from me?"

A tense silence stretched between them.

"I don't know, Ryder," Tia said honestly. "It was obviously a complicated situation. Maybe she was trying to protect you."

"Protect me from what?" Ryder barked. "From knowing I had a sibling?" He shook his head. "No. She was protecting herself and Dad," Ryder said. "She said they didn't have enough money to raise both of us."

"Was that true?"

He shrugged. "Maybe. But they claimed they paid to get me. That the McCullens sold me. That's what I thought until Cash showed up and told me the truth."

"I don't completely understand, Ryder," Tia said softly. "But they must have loved you, so give it some time."

He didn't look convinced, but the waitress appeared and he left cash to pay the bill. His phone buzzed just as she walked away.

Ryder glanced at the number then back at Tia. "It's Cash. I need to take this."

Tia decided to stop in the ladies' room while he answered the call. Her emotions were all jumbled. Hearing Ryder's story reminded her that Jordie was in someone else's arms now.

And that she had to get him back. She couldn't spend a lifetime wondering where he was and if he was safe.

RYDER INHALED THE fresh air as he stepped outside. He shouldn't have confided his story to Tia. But when she'd taken his hand and looked at him with those tender, compassionate eyes, he hadn't been able to stop himself.

His phone buzzed again. He pressed Connect. He had to get his head back in the case. "Cash?"

"Yeah. I spoke with Maddox. When he and Ray were trying to find us, they learned we were left at a church. The name Frost did come up. He was a lawyer in Sagebrush, but he died ten years ago."

"Did he have a son?"

"Yeah, his son is about our age. He took over

his father's practice." Cash paused. "Maddox questioned him about us, but he said he had no clue. Adoption records were private and sealed."

"I'll work on obtaining warrants," Ryder said. "Tia and I are going to question Frank Frost this afternoon."

"Keep us posted," Cash said.

"I will." When this case was settled, he'd meet his other brothers, too.

He ended the call, then phoned Gwen. "I need you to work on obtaining warrants for a lawyer named Frank Frost and for his files. Also, see if you can get one for his deceased father's case files."

"That'll take time."

"I think Frank Frost may be involved in the Jeffries baby kidnapping."

"Any evidence to support it?"

"That's why I need the warrants." A double-edged sword. Judges were hesitant to force situations without probable cause.

"Bonnie Cone said Frost handled her baby's

adoption. Since the name Frost surfaced regarding my adoption, I think there's a connection."

"I'll get on it ASAP."

He explained about his plan with Tia, and Gwen agreed to rush to set up a profile for the couple, complete with a background, bank information and accounts, and job history along with a cell phone he could use in dealing with the lawyer, one that couldn't be traced back to him if Frost looked. "I had Elle contact Frost's office for an appointment," Tia told him. "They emailed paperwork for us to fill out, so I'll do that before we go. I'm going to say that we've tried in vitro fertilization and it's failed several times."

"Good idea," Ryder said.

"Let's stop by Crossroads," Tia said. "I have clothes there to create a disguise."

He agreed and they drove to the center. When they arrived, Tia and Elle filled out the paperwork from Frost's office and faxed it to them, then she disappeared into a back room while Ryder checked in with the security officer he'd asked to watch the place, an ex-military guy named Blake Bowman.

"Any problems?" Ryder asked.

Bowman shook his head. "No." He lowered his voice. "The people here are something else. They're doing good work."

All thanks to Tia and her generosity.

Elle joined them, her body language exuding anxiety. "Any word about Jordie?"

"We may be on to something," he said. "How is Kelly?"

"She's settled in and seems willing to accept our help."

"Good."

Elle tucked a strand of hair behind her ear. "You are going to find Jordie, aren't you, Agent Banks?" She glanced toward the door. "Tia doesn't deserve this."

"I'm doing everything possible."

The door opened, and a woman with curly blond hair, bright green eyes and wearing a Western skirt appeared. She was almost as tall as Ryder, with big bosoms, and wore a wrist brace on one arm.

"What do you think?"

Ryder's eyes widened at the sound of Tia's voice.

He hadn't recognized her at all.

Hopefully Frost wouldn't, either.

"I didn't know it was you," he said gruffly.

She smiled. "I told you I could pull it off." She offered him a long Duster coat, hat and glasses to disguise himself, then they hurried to his SUV.

"Let me take the lead when we see Frost," he said.

She slipped something from her pocket and opened her palm to him.

Two simple gold wedding bands lay in her palm. "If we're going to inquire about adoption, we have to pose as a married couple."

Ryder considered balking, but she was right.

Still, for a single man who liked being alone, it felt odd as hell when he slid that wedding band on his third finger.

Chapter Twenty

Tia and Ryder practiced their story on the way to the lawyer's office.

Thankfully Gwen was on top of things, and Frost's personal assistant had already emailed that they had been approved and everything was in order.

Tia adjusted her wig as they parked in front of Frost's office.

"Are you sure you're up to this?" Ryder asked as they made their way up to the man's office.

Tia nodded. "I'll do whatever it takes."

Ryder gave her an encouraging smile. "You're a brave woman, Tia."

She shook her head. "Not brave. I'm a mother.

It's just what mothers do—protect their children at any cost."

"Unfortunately not all mothers are that way," Ryder said darkly. "Believe me, I've seen some shocking examples over my career."

Tia sighed. "I'm sure you have. And all your life you thought your own mother had sold you." She pressed a hand to his cheek. "Now, you know that's not true. She loved you and Cash."

She was right. Emotions clouded his expression, and he reached for the door to the lawyer's office. "Let's do this."

Tia offered him a brave smile and entered first. Playing the loving husband, Ryder kept his hand at the small of her back.

"Jared and Emma Manning," Ryder said. "I called earlier to see Mr. Frost."

The perky redhead announced their arrival to her boss. "Follow me."

Tia held on to Ryder's arm as they entered. The receptionist made introductions and offered them coffee, but she and Ryder declined.

Frank Frost was midthirties, with neatly groomed hair, a designer suit and caps that had probably cost a fortune. Framed documents on the wall chronicled his education and legal degree, along with photographs of him and an older man who resembled him, most likely his father. Another picture captured him with a leggy blonde in an evening gown posing in front of a black Mercedes. A Rolex glittered from his left arm.

Tia gritted her teeth. Had he made his money by selling babies?

Frost ran a manicured hand over his tie. "Have a seat, Mr. and Mrs. Manning, and tell me how I can help you."

Ryder started to speak, but Tia caught his arm. "Let me tell him, honey."

Ryder's gaze met hers. "Of course, sweetheart."

His look was so strained that Tia bit back a chuckle. But she focused on Frost and her act. "We've wanted a baby forever," she said earnestly. "But it hasn't been in the cards, what with my endometriosis and all. We've been through all the tests and spent a small fortune on in vitro, but it didn't work."

"I'm sorry to hear that," Frost said, injecting sympathy in his voice. "It always saddens me when folks such as yourself, who would obviously make good parents, aren't blessed in that way when others who aren't parent material spit kids out left and right."

"Thank you for understanding," Tia continued. "I was just about ready to give up, but I met this woman at the hospital when I was leaving the other day. She had the saddest story ever and told me that she'd lost her own child, but that she was adopting a baby." Tia dabbed at her eyes. "So it hit me then, that that's what we had to do."

"There are a lot of unwanted children in the world," Frost said.

"I really want an infant," Tia said. "I…just love babies and want to get a little one so he or she will bond with us from the beginning."

Frost shifted, pulling at his tie. "Infants are harder to come by and in higher demand."

"I tried to tell my wife that," Ryder said. "But she wants a baby so badly." He removed a checkbook and set it on his lap. "I'm willing to pay the adoption fees and any extra costs if we can expedite finding us a child." He tapped the checkbook. "Money is not a problem. I…have done well for myself."

Tia pressed a kiss to Ryder's cheek. "Isn't he wonderful? He's going to be an amazing father."

Frost looked back and forth between them as if searching for a lie. But Tia swiped at tears and leaned into Ryder, playing the desperate woman and adoring wife.

"Please help us," Tia whispered. "I don't think I can go on if I don't have a baby in my arms." That much was true.

Ryder curved an arm around her, pulled her to him and dropped a kiss on her head. "I promised Emma that we'd have a family," he said, his voice cracking with emotions. "You understand how difficult it is for a man to not be able to give the woman he loves everything she wants."

Frost nodded slowly. "I'm sure it's difficult."

"Not just difficult," Ryder said. "It's painful and frustrating." He opened his checkbook and reached for a pen. "Just tell me what you need to make it happen so my sweet wife here will finally get to have the child she deserves and wants."

A thick silence fell for a moment, then Frost gave a conciliatory nod. "I will see what I can do. Although it might take a few days."

Tia gripped Ryder's hand and kissed it, then shot Frost a smile of gratitude. "You have no idea how much this means to me, to us."

"I'm happy to be able to assist you." Frost shook Ryder's hand. "I'll let you know when I have a baby that suits your needs and then we'll make the arrangements."

Tia's heart pounded. She didn't want to leave without something concrete to go on. But Ryder gently pulled her to stand, keeping her close to him and playing the loving husband.

"Come on, sweetheart, it's going to be all right now." He arched a brow at Frost. "You won't let us down, will you, Mr. Frost?"

A sly grin tilted the man's face. "Just have your finances in order when I call."

"No problem." Ryder coaxed Tia to the door.

She chewed the inside of her cheek to keep from screaming at Frost and demanding that he tell her if he had her son.

Ryder pulled her out the door then back to his SUV. As soon as they climbed inside, she collapsed into the seat and closed her eyes.

RYDER'S PHONE BUZZED as they drove away. Gwen again. Hoping she had good news, he quickly connected it.

"Ryder, we just received a call through that tip line. A woman. She wouldn't talk to me, but said she needed to speak to the woman on the news."

"Maybe she'll talk to me."

"I suggested that, but she said no. It has to be Tia."

Dammit.

"Where did the call come in from?"

"I don't know, she was only on the phone for a minute. Said she wanted Tia's number."

"Did you give it to her?"

"No, I told her I'd have to speak to Tia first. But she insisted that she had information that could be helpful."

Ryder cursed. Then why the hell hadn't she just given Gwen the details? "All right. When she calls back, give her Tia's number. But keep a trace on her phone so we can track down this woman. If this is some kind of prank or if she's the one who threatened Tia earlier, I'll find her." Although the earlier caller had Tia's cell number.

Ryder ended the call then relayed the information to Tia. They were halfway back to Tia's when her phone trilled. She startled, then glanced at it and showed Ryder the display.

Unknown.

He bit back a curse, then motioned for her to answer it and place the call on speaker.

She laid the phone on the console and connected. "Hello."

Heavy breathing echoed over the line. Ryder clenched the steering wheel tighter, braced for a threat.

"Is this Tia Jeffries?"

Tia inhaled sharply. "Yes, who is this?"

"I don't want to give my name," the woman said in a low voice.

Tia twisted her mouth to the side in agitation. "Then what do you want?"

Another tense moment passed. "I don't know if this will help, but I delivered my baby at the same hospital where you did. It was six months ago, so I don't know if it's connected."

"If what's connected?" Tia asked.

"I'm a single mother," the woman continued. "I was down on my luck, moneywise, and lost my job a few weeks before the baby was due."

Ryder and Tia exchanged a questioning glance. Where was she going with her story?

"Anyway, when I was in the hospital in labor, this nurse came in to be my coach. At first he was nice and supportive, but he said he heard me telling the nurse at check-in that I had no insurance and that I was going to raise the baby alone."

Tia took a deep breath. "Go on."

"That's when things got odd."

"What do you mean odd?"

"He asked me if I'd considered giving my baby up for adoption."

Tia paled. "Had you?"

"No...well, maybe it occurred to me, but that was only because I was so broke and was afraid I couldn't take care of my child on my own. But I didn't think I could do it." The woman hesitated, her breathing agitated again.

"What happened?" Tia asked.

"I told him I'd think about it." She cleared her throat. "But once I held little Catherine in my arms, I knew I couldn't let her go. Then the nurse came in to visit me in the hospital room and pressured me. Said he knew someone who wanted a baby really badly, that we could go through a private adoption and I'd be compensated well enough to take care of my hospital bills and set me up for the future."

Ryder's blood ran cold.

"Then what?" Tia asked, her voice shaky with emotions.

"I told him no, again. And again. Then the day I brought my little girl home, he showed up at my house. It freaked me out, and I threatened to call the police if he contacted me again."

"What did he do then?" Tia asked.

"He got angry. But I held firm. When I picked up the phone to call 911, he left."

"Have you heard from him since?"

"No. But when I saw your story, it reminded me of how much that experience disturbed me. I mean, he knew where I lived. That I was alone.

He even made me feel bad, that I was being selfish for raising a child on my own."

Tia rubbed her forehead. "You said *he*. It was a male nurse."

"Yes, his name was Richard." Her voice wavered. "Maybe I was just paranoid, but I...just thought it might be important."

"Thank you," Tia said. "Actually, Richard was one of my nurses when I went into the hospital, too."

Ryder swung the SUV off the side of the road and parked. Tia thanked the woman and asked her to call if she thought of anything else.

As soon as they disconnected, he phoned Gwen. "I need an address and everything you can find on a nurse named Richard Blotter."

TIA RACKED HER brain to remember if Richard had mentioned adoption to her.

She'd been half-delirious with excitement and pain that night when she had arrived at the ER.

He had helped her into the wheelchair and

gotten her settled into a labor room. When she'd told him she had no labor coach, he assured her he'd help her through the process, but then Amy had stepped in.

"Tia?" Ryder's gruff voice broke into her thoughts. "What do you know about Richard Blotter?"

She massaged her temple, where a headache was starting to pulse. "Not much. He was nice to me, and seemed caring. But that night was chaotic."

"He knew you were a single mother?"

Tia nodded. "Yes, he was actually ending his shift, but he must have stayed, because he came by to see me after Jordie was born."

"So he knew you lived alone?"

"Yes." Bits and pieces of their conversation trickled through her mind. "He said he wasn't married, but he wanted to have a family some-day. That he chose nursing because he liked to help people. He especially liked labor and delivery because he enjoyed being part of such a happy day for people."

"Did he seem suspicious to you? Like anything was off?"

Tia struggled to recall specifics. "Not really. He said he was raised by a single mother, and that it had been hard on her and him. That he always wanted a father." She hesitated. "I told him I wanted my baby to have a father, too, but the father wasn't interested."

Horror struck her.

She had been scared and in pain and nervous over the delivery and had spilled her guts about those fears.

Had Richard befriended her so he could gain access to her baby?

Chapter Twenty-One

Ryder gritted his teeth as the pieces clicked together in his mind.

Richard Blotter grew up in a single-parent home, missed having a father and resented it—perhaps he had projected his own bitterness on Tia and other women who chose to raise babies on their own.

The profile fit.

He also had access to patient files, worked in the labor and delivery unit and had personal contact with Tia. Bonnie had delivered at the same hospital, lost her baby and wanted another child.

But if Blotter was trying to place kids in two-parent homes, why would he have helped Bonnie adopt a baby when her husband had left her?

Unless he didn't know about the separation…

"Did Blotter ever call you at home or drop by to see you?"

Tia shook her head no. "But he could have found out where I lived."

"I know." Ryder punched the number for the hospital. "This is Agent Ryder Banks with the FBI. Is Richard Blotter on duty today?"

"Just a moment, please. I'll check," the receptionist said.

Tia bounced her leg up and down in a nervous gesture. Ryder rubbed her arm to soothe her.

"Agent Banks, actually, he was scheduled to work today, but he didn't show."

"Did he call in?"

"No, and that's odd. He's usually very dependable. Maybe there was a mix-up and he didn't realize he was on the schedule."

Or maybe he suspected his days were numbered, that the police were on to him.

"All right, if he shows up, please give me a call."

"May I ask what this is about? Do you think something happened to Richard?"

"I can't say at this point," Ryder said. "Just please let me know if he shows up at the hospital."

He checked his text messages. Gwen had sent him Blotter's home address. "He's not at the hospital today," he told Tia as he turned the SUV around and began to follow his GPS. "We're going to his house."

"I can't believe that Richard would do this," Tia said. "He seemed so nice and caring. I… trusted him."

"He was a nurse at the hospital," Ryder said. "You had no reason not to trust him."

"But I should have picked up on something."

Ryder blew a breath through his teeth. "People can fool us, Tia. Believe me, I've dealt with sociopaths who can lie without blinking an eye.

Besides, you met him when you were vulnerable."

"I should have been smarter," Tia said, anger lacing her tone. "I let him get close and he kidnapped my child."

"We don't know that yet," Ryder said, although his gut instinct told him they were on the right track.

Tia shifted and turned to look out the window as they drove. "I don't know whether to wish that he was involved or to hope that he wasn't."

"You're strong, Tia. If he is, at least we're getting closer to finding your baby."

He pressed the accelerator and sped toward Blotter's.

GUILT NAGGED AT Tia as Ryder drove. If her conversation with Richard was the reason he'd abducted Jordie, she'd never forgive herself.

She mentally replayed the night she'd given birth over and over in her head. Jordie had been a normal delivery—alert, his Apgar score high.

She'd nursed him right away and kept him in the room with her all night.

She hadn't wanted him out of her sight.

Amy had assured her that her reaction was normal, that a lot of first-time mothers were paranoid about their newborn being away from them for even a moment.

She'd been right to be paranoid.

She'd just thought she and Jordie were safe in her own house.

They should have been, dammit.

Ryder veered into an apartment complex a mile from the hospital.

He checked the address, then wove through the parking lot in search of Blotter's building.

"There it is." Ryder gestured to an end unit. The parking spots in front of it were empty, a sign Blotter wasn't home.

"I'm going to check it out. You can wait here if you want." He opened the car door and Tia jumped out, close on his heels.

Anger surged through Tia, pumping her adrenaline, and she removed her wig and dropped it on the seat. She wanted to confront Richard herself.

"Let me do the talking," Ryder said when they reached the door.

Tia nodded, although if Richard admitted he'd abducted her baby, she couldn't promise that she wouldn't tear his eyes out.

Ryder rang the doorbell, his gaze scanning the parking lot while they waited. Afternoon was turning to evening, and the lot was nearly empty.

Ryder punched the bell again, then pushed at the door. To her surprise, the door squeaked open.

Ryder motioned for her to stay behind him, then he removed his weapon from his holster. "Mr. Blotter, FBI Special Agent Ryder Banks."

Tia peeked past him. The foyer was empty. Ryder inched inside. "Mr. Blotter?"

Silence echoed back.

Holding his gun at the ready, Ryder moved forward. Tia stayed behind him, her gaze scanning the living room, which held a faded couch and chair. A small wooden table occupied the breakfast nook, paper cups and fast-food wrappers littering it.

No sign of a baby anywhere.

Ryder checked the bathroom and bedroom. "Clear. He's not here."

Tia stepped into the small bedroom. A faded spread, dingy curtains—no sign of Blotter. Ryder opened the closet door, and disappointment filled Tia.

No clothes inside.

She checked the dresser drawers. Empty.

Richard Blotter was gone.

"DAMMIT," RYDER SAID. "It looks like he left quickly."

"You think he knew we were coming?" Tia asked.

Ryder shrugged. "I don't know how he could. Not unless the nurse at the hospital gave him a heads-up we were asking about him." He phoned

Gwen. "Get a BOLO out on Richard Blotter. He's cleaned out his apartment."

"On it," Gwen said. "I'm looking at his bank account now, Ryder. He cleaned it out, too."

"Were there any suspicious transactions before today?"

Tapping on computer keys echoed in the background. "He made a couple of big deposits over the last four years but quickly moved the money into an offshore account."

Could those have been payoffs for kidnapping babies or convincing single mothers to choose the adoption route?

"What about another house or property that he owns?"

"I don't see anything." She hummed beneath her breath. "Wait a minute, he has a sister."

That could be helpful. "What's her name?"

"Judy Kinley," Gwen said.

"Judy?" He glanced at Tia and saw her skin turn ashen.

"Yes, she lives—"

"Across the street from Tia Jeffries." Ryder's pulse jumped. "Find out everything you can on her and Blotter. If there's a second address or other family members, let me know. And examine both their phone records."

If Blotter and his sister were working with Frost or with another party, they might find a clue in their contacts.

Tia was staring at him with a sick expression when he ended the call.

"Judy is Richard's sister?"

Ryder nodded.

"She never mentioned that her brother worked at the hospital," Tia said. "She came into my house and pretended to be my friend. She brought me food and a gift when Jordie was born." She gasped. "Oh, my gosh, she even brought me a dessert that day. I had some that night. Do you think she put something in it to make me sleep?"

Ryder silently cursed. "It might explain why

you didn't wake up when Blotter came in. And why there were no signs of a break-in on the window," Ryder said.

Tia dropped her face into her hands. "Because she was in the nursery. She must have unlocked the window that day she visited me and Jordie." Tia pressed a hand to her chest on a pained sigh. "It's all my fault. I welcomed her in. I let her hold my baby."

Ryder rushed to console her. "This was not your fault," he said firmly. "These people are predators."

Anger replaced the hurt on her face. "We need to go to Judy's."

Ryder's gaze swept the room. He doubted she was home. If Blotter had skipped, she'd probably left with him.

"Help me look around here before we go. Maybe he left a clue to tell us where he went."

"I'll check the kitchen," she said.

Tia raced to the other room while he dug

through the drawers and closet. But Blotter had cleaned them out as well, leaving no sign as to his plan.

TIA HOPED TO find something in the kitchen, an address or contact they could trace to her son, but the drawers and cabinets were empty.

Pain and hurt cut through her.

They had to find Richard and Judy. They were the key to her son.

Ryder appeared a second later. “Nothing in there. Gwen’s searching their contacts, bank records, history.”

Tia rushed to the door. “Let’s go. Maybe Richard hasn’t gotten to Judy yet.”

They hurried outside, and Ryder raced toward Tia’s neighborhood. She mentally beat herself up all the way.

How could she have been so stupid? She’d trusted Darren, and he’d deceived her. She’d trusted the hospital, the staff and nurses, but one of them had conspired to take her son. Then she'd trusted her neighbor who seemed friendly and helpful.

That was one of the worst deceptions. How could a woman do that to another woman?

Judy had taken betrayal to a new level—she'd consoled Tia the very night Jordie had disappeared.

No wonder Judy had been so quick to rush over. She'd known what was coming. She'd been watching the house, had probably alerted her brother when the house was quiet. When Tia had turned out the light.

Maybe she'd even stalled when she'd come to Tia's rescue to give her brother more time to make his escape with her son.

Ryder took the turn into the neighborhood on two wheels. He screeched into Judy's driveway, and they both hit the ground running.

Ryder gestured for her to wait behind him, then he drew his gun and held it at his side as he pounded on the door. "Judy? It's Agent Banks. We need to talk."

Tia checked the garage, but Judy's car was not inside.

Her heart sank. "Her car's gone, Ryder."

His jaw tightened. He knocked again then jiggled the door. Just like Blotter's, the door swung open. Ryder stormed in, Tia behind him, calling Judy's name.

The empty bookshelves looked stark now, a reminder that Judy hadn't added any personal touches to the place. No family photos or mementos.

Now Tia understood the reason.

Ryder raced through the house searching while Tia checked the kitchen drawers and desk. She fumbled through a few unpaid bills, then found a small note pad with several pages ripped out.

An envelope caught her eye, and she pulled it out and gasped. Several pictures of her when she was pregnant were tucked inside.

She checked the drawer again, hoping for an address or phone number of someone Judy or Richard might be working with.

Her fingers brushed something wedged inside the top desk drawer, the end caught. She stooped down and gently pulled at it until it came loose.

Rage shot through her. It was a photo of Jordie the day she'd brought him home from the hospital.

Ryder's boots pounded on the staircase as he rushed down. "Nothing upstairs."

Tia's hand trembled as she tossed the picture on top of the desk. "I was so stupid. She was watching me all along."

Ryder cursed and reached for the photo, but suddenly the sound of something crashing through the window jarred them both. A popping sound followed.

Then smoke began to fill the room.

Chapter Twenty-Two

Ryder dragged Tia outside into the fresh air as smoke billowed into the room. He pulled her beneath a cottonwood, and they leaned against it, panting for breath.

Tires screeched. Instantly alert, he scanned the yard and street and spotted a dark car racing down the road.

Did it belong to the person who'd thrown that smoke bomb in the house?

"What was that?" Tia said on a cough.

"Someone who doesn't want us finding the truth," Ryder said, jaw clenched.

Tia pushed her hair from her face. "Judy Kinley and Richard Blotter are definitely involved."

"I agree."

Ryder removed his phone to call 911, but a siren wailed and a fire truck careened around the corner. Someone on the street must have seen the explosion and called.

The fire engine wheeled into the driveway and firefighters jumped into action. "Are you okay?" Ryder asked Tia.

"Yes, go talk to them."

One of the firemen met him on the lawn. "What happened?"

Ryder explained.

"Anyone hurt or inside?"

"No. I'm going to call a crime unit to process the inside of the house, though. I believe the woman who was living here was involved in a baby kidnapping."

The fireman lifted his helmet slightly, expression dark, then gave a nod and went to join the others. Ryder phoned for the crime unit, then made his way back to Tia as they waited.

She paced the yard, looking shell-shocked. "I can't believe Judy would do this to me. Why?"

Ryder shrugged. "Maybe she was protecting her brother or needed money."

"But who did they give my baby to?"

He wished to hell he knew. "We'll find him, Tia. We're getting closer."

"If Richard was involved, do you think someone else at the hospital knew?"

Good question. "Let's go back to the hospital and see." Maybe by then Gwen would have something on Richard and his sister, like an address where they might be hiding out. She was supposed to be checking their prints against the matchbook he'd found outside the baby's nursery.

The crime team arrived ten minutes later, and Ryder explained the situation to the chief investigator while Tia walked across the street to her house to change from her disguise.

"I want the place fingerprinted," he said. "Then let's compare the prints to the matchbook we found outside the nursery." He had a feeling Blotter and Judy were accomplices.

Frost still ranked high on his list as the leader.

One of them might be able to point them to the person who actually had Jordie.

TIA BATTLED NERVES as she and Ryder entered the hospital. Each time she walked through the door, the memory of giving birth to her son returned. She had been so proud when she'd carried him home that day, so elated and full of plans for the future.

That future looked dismal without Jordie in it.

Ryder went straight to the nurses' station. Hilda, the charge nurse, waved to her. "Tia, I saw the news story," Hilda said. "Is there any word?"

"Not yet." Tia motioned for Hilda to step aside and they slipped into the break room while Ryder canvassed the other staff for information on Richard.

"Hilda, I have reason to think that Richard

Blotter might have been involved. Did you ever see or hear him do anything suspicious?"

Hilda's eyes widened. "No, he was always so helpful, especially with the single mothers." Alarm flashed across her face as if she realized the implications. "Are you suggesting he was friendly because he was up to something?"

Tia nodded. "I don't think he was working alone, though. His sister lived across from me. I think she was watching me and unlocked the window in the nursery so he could come in and take Jordie."

"But why would they do such a thing?" Hilda asked.

That was the big question. "I don't know yet," Tia said. "But some people are willing to pay a lot to adopt a baby."

Hilda gasped.

Tia's stomach knotted. "Was Richard close to anyone here at the hospital? Did he have a girlfriend?"

Hilda scowled and peered down the hall. "Not that I know of."

Tia bit her tongue in frustration. "Is Amy here today?"

"She just left, sweetie." Hilda's phone buzzed, and she checked the number. "I have to get this. I'm praying for you, Tia."

Tia thanked her and followed her back to the nurses' station. She punched Amy's number then left a message asking Amy to call her.

Amy had worked more closely with Richard than Hilda. Maybe she knew something about him that could help.

RYDER'S NEWLY ISSUED phone vibrated as he ended his conversation with an orderly who stated that he'd always thought Blotter showed a peculiar interest in the single mothers. He'd thought Blotter was interested in striking up a romance, but it was an odd place to look for female companionship.

Ryder agreed with that.

The phone vibrated again. Frost's number showed up on the screen. Surprised to hear something so quickly, he hesitated. Frost might be on to them.

"Jared Manning speaking."

"Yes, Mr. Manning, I reviewed your information and everything seems to be in order."

"Great. When do you think you'll have a baby for us?"

"Actually, that's the reason I'm calling. Typically it takes months to find an infant, but it just so happens that we were placing a baby today, but the couple we were working with backed out. So, it may seem sudden, but if you and your wife are interested, we could arrange for you to take this child."

Sweat beaded on Ryder's neck. He wasn't buying the man's story. Maybe Frost had checked out the phony bank account and decided the Mannings had more money than the other couple so his profit would be larger.

Whatever, he couldn't turn down this opportunity. "Of course we're interested. Is it a boy or a girl?"

A pregnant pause. "I believe it's a little girl. I didn't think you were particular about the sex."

"We're not," Ryder said, careful to keep his tone neutral. "I just wanted to tell my wife. She's going to be so excited. I'm sure she'll want to pick up some clothes and girly things."

"Good. I'm glad. Now we have some details to work out."

"Just tell me what you need," Ryder said.

"My secretary will send you an account number for a wire transfer and the amount. Once that's taken care of, we'll schedule a time and place for you to pick up the baby."

"How soon will this happen?"

"Since we already had this adoption arranged, the placement can happen tonight. That is, unless that's too soon."

"No, tonight is great. I can't wait to tell my wife."

"Good. You'll receive the details shortly. I

hope you and your wife and the little girl will be very happy."

Ryder assured him they would be, then stared at the phone in silence when the man hung up.

He hurried toward Tia. "Frost just called. He has a baby for us."

Hope lit Tia's eyes. "A little boy?"

He shook his head. He'd probably already placed Jordie. "A baby girl. But if we catch him in the act, we can force him to talk."

Renewed determination mingled with disgust on Tia's face. "When do we get her?"

Ryder's phone dinged with a text. He quickly skimmed for details.

"Tonight. Eight o'clock. I'll have Gwen wire money into his account now."

His mind churned. If they were about to crack a baby stealing/selling ring, he wanted to take Frost and whoever else was involved down. His first thought was to call Maddox, the sheriff of Pistol Whip.

But he'd never even met the man.

This was not how he wanted to meet, either.

So he phoned his boss. Statham would send backup with no questions asked.

AN HOUR LATER, Tia dressed again in her disguise. Tonight she was no longer Tia Jeffries—she was Emma Manning.

Looking to adopt a child.

Granted, she'd hoped the baby that the lawyer would bring was her own son, but at least they were one step closer to finding him.

If Frost was selling babies to the highest bidder, they would catch him and put him away.

She certainly didn't want any other mother to suffer the pain she'd felt the past few days.

Ryder donned his disguise as well. They didn't want anyone to immediately recognize him and run. Anxiety filled Tia as they drove to Frost's office to finalize the paperwork.

He wasn't in the office, but his receptionist handed him the documents and they signed them, anxious to complete the exchange.

When the lawyer's personal assistant left the room, Ryder photographed the documents and sent a copy to the lab for analysis.

Then they went to the outdoor café next door to pick up the baby. She and Ryder had both agreed that was an odd place for an adoption exchange, that it indicated something fishy, but they had to follow through, pretend to be the desperate couple who asked no questions but paid to get what they wanted.

Ryder visually scanned the parking lot as he parked. "Are you ready?"

Tia nodded. He'd insisted they bring a rental van in case they were being watched. Richard and Judy might recognize Tia's. She had insisted Ryder install the car seat. Whoever this baby belonged to, she intended to protect the child at all costs.

Ryder squeezed her hand. "Remember, play it cool. We'll wait until the child is handed over and then move in to ask questions or make an arrest."

"Do you think Frost or Richard Blotter will show?"

"I have no idea what to expect, but we have to be prepared for anything."

Tia braced herself and adjusted her wig. She'd never felt so alone.

Except for Ryder. He was here.

She'd hang on to him as long as possible. And when she got Jordie back, she'd once again learn to manage on her own.

"How are we supposed to know who we're meeting?" she asked.

Ryder gestured toward the entrance and then asked for a table. "Frost's assistant sent our photograph to whoever is bringing the baby."

Tia fidgeted with her purse, trying to act normal, but her pulse was racing. Ryder threw his arm around her, nuzzling her neck, perpetuating the image of a young couple in love as they made their way to the hostess's station.

Ryder pointed out a corner table toward the

back of the outdoor seating area. "We want that table."

Tia realized he'd chosen it to give them a good view of the entrance so he could look for the person they were supposed to meet.

She draped herself around him as they walked to the table, half faking the kisses yet needing his strength to help her through the nerve-racking ordeal. When they sat, the waitress immediately deposited water on the table and took coffee orders.

Ryder positioned his chair to watch the entrance and pulled her close to him again, twining his fingers with hers. She stared at their laced fingers—her hand so small in his, his so large and callused yet so tender, and a wealth of emotions swelled in her throat.

Suddenly he stiffened, and she jerked her gaze to the door. Her heart stalled in her chest.

Amy, the young labor nurse who'd befriended her, appeared, holding an infant.

"My God, not Amy," Tia whispered.

Amy scanned the seating area, shifting back and forth, her movements jittery. A second later, she looked at Ryder and must have recognized him.

Panic streaked her expression, then she turned and ran.

Chapter Twenty-Three

"Amy?" Tia rose to go after the young woman, but Amy had disappeared.

Ryder shot up. "I'm going after her!"

He jumped the gate to the patio and Tia jogged to the gate entrance, pushed it open and followed. Amy was running across the street toward a white SUV, clutching the baby to her.

Ryder caught up to her and cornered her by the vehicle. Tia's breath rasped out as she wove between cars.

Shock mingled with hurt and disbelief. Tia removed her wig and Amy gasped.

"You took my son?" Tia cried.

Amy shook her head in denial. The baby

started to cry and she jiggled the infant in her arms, trying to shush it. "No, I didn't do it, Tia. I swear."

Ryder folded his arms, his big body blocking her from escaping and pressing her against the side of the SUV.

"Who does this child belong to?" Ryder asked, his tone hard.

Tears blurred Amy's eyes. "A teenager. She gave her up for adoption."

"Just like I supposedly did," Tia snapped.

Amy's face contorted in pain.

"Where's my son?" Tia shouted.

"You have to believe me, Tia," Amy said. "I… didn't take Jordie. I swear."

"Then what's going on?" Ryder demanded.

Amy trembled, the baby crying louder. She patted its back, but Tia reached out and took the infant. Her arms had felt empty for so long. This little girl wasn't Jordie, but she could comfort her until they brought her home to her mother.

"Explain," Ryder said sharply.

Amy wiped at her eyes. "I…I swear I didn't know about Jordie or anything about babies being kidnapped."

"Yet here you are," Ryder said with no sympathy.

"I got a call, was told to drop this baby off with its adopted parents."

"Who called you?" Ryder asked.

"Richard Blotter," Amy said. "He…threatened me, threatened my little girl." More tears trickled down her cheeks. "You know my daughter is handicapped. She needs surgery. I didn't have the money…"

"He paid you to steal babies from the nursery," Ryder cut in.

"No." She sucked in a sharp breath. "A while back, I caught Richard Blotter hacking into patient files. He said he worked with a lawyer who handled adoptions. I threatened to tell the hospital that he was violating patient confidentiality, but he assured me he was only helping mothers and families by connecting them with the lawyer. I thought it was legitimate."

Amy looked miserable. "I had to do something to help Linnie. She needs braces to straighten her legs so one day she can walk. I…just wanted to give her a normal life, as normal as she could have."

The baby had quieted in Tia's arms as she swayed back and forth.

"But you eventually figured out what was happening?" Ryder asked.

Amy gulped. "I heard Richard on the phone a couple of days ago. He sounded upset, nervous. He said they had to lie low, that the police were asking questions." She twisted her purse strap between her fingers. "That's when I realized what had happened."

"Then why didn't you come forward and tell me?" Tia cried.

"I confronted Richard, but he said if I told I'd be arrested for my part, that I'd go to jail for aiding in a kidnapping." She gave Tia an imploring look. “I couldn’t go to jail, not when my little girl needs me.”

Compassion for the woman’s situation filled Tia, but hurt over Amy’s betrayal overpowered it. “So you just kept quiet and let them take my baby. Where is he, Amy? Where is Jordie?”

Amy’s face wilted again and she shook her head. “I don’t know, Tia. I…honestly don’t know.”

“I’M SORRY, MISS YOST,” Ryder said. “But you’re going to have to come with me until we sort this out.”

Amy shot Tia a panicked look. “But I’m supposed to go home to Linnie.”

“Who’s with her now?” Tia asked.

“My mother.” Amy’s voice cracked. “She’ll be devastated if I go to jail. And if I lose my job, I can’t support us.”

“Let’s take it one step at a time.” Ryder guided Amy to the rental van. Tia carried the baby, soothing the infant with her soft voice.

She strapped the baby into the car seat in the back beside Amy, who was staring into space, ashen-faced and terrified.

Ryder needed a safe place to leave her, but he didn't want to take her to Sheriff Gaines. He considered the McCullens, but this wasn't the way he wanted to meet his brothers. He still had to bring Frost in for questioning and find Blotter and Judy.

He drove to the FBI office instead then escorted Amy to an interrogation room. "Do you have information on the mother of that baby?" Ryder asked.

She shook her head no. "I was just told that she'd signed away her rights and that another couple wanted her."

He pushed her again for more on Frost, but she didn't seem to know anything else helpful.

A kind woman named Constance from the Department of Family Services arrived to take the baby until they sorted out the custody issue.

"I'm sorry, Tia, really," Amy said for the dozenth time.

"Just cooperate and tell the police whatever you know," Tia said. "I don't want what happened to me to happen to anyone else."

Ryder's chest clenched. Even though Tia was suffering, she still had compassion for Amy. She was an unusual woman.

"My little girl needs me," Amy said in a pained whisper.

"Tia's baby needs her, too," Ryder said. "Cooperate and we'll see what we can work out."

They left Amy in federal custody and the baby with Constance then drove back toward Frost's office.

"I'm sorry your friend was involved," Ryder said.

Tia muttered a sarcastic sound. "It seems like everyone I meet lies to me." She touched Ryder's arm. "Promise me you won't do that. If you find out something about Jordie, promise you'll tell me no matter what."

Ryder didn't want to be the bearer of bad news. He wasn't giving up now, either. "I promise."

She relaxed slightly, and he sped into the lawyer's office parking lot. Although he was gone earlier, Frost's Mercedes was in the parking lot now.

Ryder led the way, anxious to get this bastard and make him talk. Early evening shadows played across the parking lot, accentuating the fact that most everyone had gone home for the day.

He snatched the warrants he got at the FBI office from his pocket as he reached the office door, then gave a quick rap on the door and pushed it open. He paused in the entryway to listen for sounds that Frost was inside or had a client but heard no voices. Only the faint sound of a familiar machine.

A paper shredder.

Adrenaline pumping, he rushed through the reception area, following the noise. Frost was in the file room behind the shredder, feeding files into it.

"Stop, Mr. Frost. I'm Special Agent Ryder Banks." Ryder waved the envelope. "I have warrants for your files."

Frost shifted, then reached down. Ryder thought he was going for the files, but Frost lifted a pistol and fired at them.

Tia screamed and ducked behind the door. Ryder pulled his weapon and fired back, hitting Frost in the chest. Frost grunted in shock, dropped his gun and collapsed to the floor.

Ryder kept his gun aimed on the man as he rushed toward him. Frost was reaching for his pistol again when Ryder made it to him, but Ryder kicked it out of the way.

"It's over, Frost," Ryder barked.

Tia ran up behind him. "Where's my son, you bastard?"

Frost coughed, his eyes closing then opening again.

Ryder stooped down and grabbed the man around the neck. "Where's the baby?"

Frost gasped and tried to speak, choking for a breath. Blood gushed from his chest wound, soaking his white designer shirt. Then his eyes rolled back in his head and he faded into unconsciousness.

Ryder released the man abruptly. "Don't you dare die, you bastard."

Tia dropped to her knees and shook the man. "Wake up and tell me where my baby is!"

But Frost's only response was to gurgle up blood.

Ryder cursed, afraid it was too late, and called for an ambulance.

TIA FOUGHT DESPAIR as the paramedics loaded the lawyer's unconscious body onto the stretcher and into the ambulance. Ryder instantly went to work searching the files while the crime unit began processing the office space and sorting through the shredded documents.

Tia looked over Ryder's shoulder into the file cabinet. "Anything on Jordie?"

"Not yet." He offered her a smile of encouragement. "But don't give up. We still have mountains of papers to sort through, plus we need to search his computer."

Tia tried to hang on to hope. They couldn't have come this far and not find her baby.

Although if Frost had destroyed the documents pertaining to Jordie and he died, and they didn't find Richard Blotter, her son might be lost to her forever.

Chapter Twenty-Four

Ryder hoped the search of Frost's files would turn up an address for the person who had Tia's son, but no such luck. There was a list of other adoptions, which appeared to be legitimate, but he turned them over to the Bureau's unit that worked with the National Center for Missing and Exploited Children—NCMEC—to verify the adoptions and their legitimacy.

He and Tia sat in silence in the waiting room of the hospital, their nerves raw. A few minutes later, a doctor appeared with a grave expression on his face. "I'm sorry, but Mr. Frost didn't make it."

Tia sagged against him, devastated. Their only lead was gone.

"We're still looking at his computer, and if we find Blotter, he may have the information we need."

She nodded against him, although her despair bled into his own. He didn't want this case to end without answers.

He wrapped his arms around her. "I'm driving you home to get some rest."

"I want to do another press conference," Tia said. "Tonight."

Ryder debated on the wisdom of the idea, but what did they have to lose?

He phoned the station and spoke with Jesse, the anchorwoman who'd interviewed Tia before. She was anxious for more of the story and agreed to the late-night segment.

If Ryder had exposed a major baby-selling ring, the public had a right to know. They also needed eyes searching for Blotter and his sister, Judy.

They stopped for Tia to change out of her disguise. She looked exhausted and sad, but she held her head up and faced the camera with a brave face.

Ryder spoke first. "Tonight we have information regarding the missing Jeffries baby, although we do not have the baby back in custody." He explained about the lawyer's alleged adoption setup and his theory about Blotter and his sister serving as accomplices.

"If anyone has seen or had contact with Mr. Blotter or Ms. Kinley, please phone our tip line." The station displayed pictures of the man and his sister. "Or if you have information regarding Mr. Frost and his adoption practices, please come forward."

Tia clenched the microphone with a white-knuckled grip. "I'm Tia Jeffries and I'm pleading with you again. I believe these people abducted my son. It's possible that whoever adopted my baby isn't aware that he was stolen from his own bed, from his mother. If that is the case, there will be no repercussions. I just want my son back safely."

She wiped at a tear but managed to maintain control as the anchorwoman summarized the story and repeated the number for the tip line.

"Good luck, Miss Jeffries." Jesse gave her a hug.

Tia thanked her and Ryder drove her home. When they reached her house, Tia rushed inside.

She darted into the bathroom and shut the door, then he heard the shower water kick on and her sobs followed.

TIA FELT LIMP when she climbed from the shower. She dried off and combed through her wet hair on autopilot, numb from the day's events. She yanked on a tank top and pajama pants and left the bathroom in a daze.

Ryder was standing in the living room, a bottle of whiskey in front of him along with two glasses. He raised a brow and she nodded. Why not?

Maybe it would dull the pain for a while. Maybe when she woke up tomorrow, Jordie would be home in his crib and her life would be normal again.

Then Ryder would be gone.

She wanted her son back. But she realized she didn't necessarily want Ryder to leave.

Not a good sign.

He handed her the whiskey, and she swirled it around in the glass, lost in the deep amber color and the intoxicating smell.

Ryder tossed his drink down, then pressed his lips into a thin line. "We're not giving up, Tia. Don't think that."

His words soothed her battered soul. But she wanted more. His touch. His kiss. His mouth on hers, his lips driving away the pain with pleasure.

She sipped her drink. "I trust you, Ryder. I know you'll find him."

He slowly walked toward her. "You are the strongest woman I've ever known."

"I'm not strong," Tia said in a hoarse whisper.

"You are." He reached out and tucked a strand of damp hair behind her ear. His movement was so gentle and tender that her throat closed.

Yet her heart opened to him, and her body screamed with need. Unable to resist, she placed her hand against his cheek. His skin was tanned, rough with dark beard stubble, his eyes liquid pools of male hunger, desire and strength.

She needed that strength tonight.

She finished her drink, then pushed the glass into his hand.

"Another?"

She shook her head no. "I don't want a drink."

He swallowed hard, his jaw tightening as she traced a thumb over his lips.

"Tia?"

"Shh, don't talk." Her body hummed to life with the desire to be closer to him.

She gave in to it, stood on tiptoe and pressed her lips to his. The first touch was raw, his breath filled with hunger. Her skin tingled as he deepened the kiss.

She whispered his name on a breath as he plunged his tongue into her mouth, and she tilted her head back, offering him free rein on her neck and throat as passion drove her to pull him closer.

She fumbled with the buttons of his shirt, and he brushed her cheek with the back of his hand, then lower to trace over her shoulder and down to her hip.

He pressed her into the vee of his thighs, his thick sex building against her belly, a sign that he wanted her just as she wanted him.

That was all she needed.

She was tired of hurting all the time.

For this one minute in time, she wanted to feel pleasure. Pushing the guilt aside, she clutched his arms and pressed her breasts against his chest.

Her nipples throbbed, stiffening to peaks, the warm tingle of electricity in her womb a reminder that she hadn't felt this way about a man in a long time.

She didn't bother to question what was happening. Life made no sense. All she'd known was pain for days.

Tomorrow the pain would be back.

But tonight, Ryder could alleviate it.

EVERY OUNCE OF Ryder's ethical training ordered him to stop. To walk away.

But his body didn't seem to be listening to his brain.

Instead, the hunger inside him surged raw and primal, driving him to hold Tia closer, to stroke her back and shoulders, to brush her breast with one hand until he felt her chest rise and fall with her sharp intake of breath.

He deepened the kiss, savoring the heat between them as she met his tongue thrust for thrust. Her hands raked over his shoulders and back, her touch stirring his body's need.

He shifted, his erection throbbing against her belly and aching to be inside her warm heat.

She coaxed him to the bedroom until they stood by her bed. Soft moonlight spilled through the room, painting her in an ethereal glow. Yet that glow accentuated the paleness of her skin and the sadness in her eyes.

He took a deep breath and forced his hands to be still, to look into her face. "I won't take advantage of you," he said gruffly.

Her gaze met his, turmoil and pain and some other emotion he couldn't define flaring strong. "Then I'll take advantage of you."

With one quick shove she pushed him onto the bed.

His chest clenched. "Tia?"

"Shh." She pushed him to his back then crawled on top of him, straddling him and moving against him in a sensual move that sent white-hot heat through him.

He cupped her face with his hands and drew her to him for another kiss. Lips met and melded.

Tongues mated and danced. His hands raced over her body as she tore at the buttons on his shirt.

She shoved the garment aside and the two of them frantically removed it, then she tossed it to the floor. Her hands made a quick foray over his chest, making his lungs explode with the need for air.

"You're beautiful, Tia," he murmured. God, she deserved better than this.

She kissed him again, then lowered her head and trailed kisses and tongue lashes along his neck. She teased and bit at his nipples, stroking his sex with one hand while she worked his belt and zipper with the other.

He wanted her naked before he exploded, dammit.

He slowed her hands, then settled her hips over his sex, moving her gently so he could cup her breasts in his hands. They were full, round and fit into his palms.

He kneaded them then lifted his head, pushed

her tank top up and closed his lips over one ripe nipple. She moaned, threw her head back and clung to him.

He flipped her to her back then straddled her this time, loving both breasts with his hands and mouth, her moans of pleasure eliciting his own.

He trailed his tongue down her abdomen, then shoved her pajama bottoms off and spread her legs. She clawed at his back, but he wanted her, sweet and succulent in his mouth, hard and fast below him.

Pushing her legs farther apart, he drove his tongue to her sweet heat and suckled her. She groaned, writhing beneath him as he plunged his tongue deep inside her and tasted her release.

The sound of her crying his name as she came apart sent erotic sensations through him, and he rolled sideways long enough to discard his jeans and pull on a condom.

Then he rose above her, kneed her legs apart again and looked into her eyes.

The raw passion and pleasure on her face stole his breath.

He wanted to see her look like that again and again.

She closed her hand around his thick length and guided him inside her. He moaned her name and found his way home.

TIA CURLED INTO Ryder's arms, closed her eyes and savored the sensual aftermath of their love-making.

Although guilt niggled at her. How could she enjoy herself when her baby was still missing?

Still, her body quivered with erotic sensations, and she clung to him as if hiding in his arms could erase reality.

Finally she drifted into sleep. But sometime later, a ringing phone jarred her awake.

Ryder rolled from the bed, snatched his cell phone and answered. "Yeah? Okay. I'll be right there."

He reached for his shirt as he ended the call.

"Who was that?" Tia asked.

"Gwen. Someone spotted a man they think is Blotter at a motel near the airport. I'm going after him."

Tia pushed at the covers. "I'll go, too."

Ryder eased down on the bed beside her. "No, Tia, stay here and rest. He didn't have the baby with him. He might be dangerous."

Ryder's touch reminded her of their night of lovemaking, the frenzied, harried hunger, the gentle touches, the pleasure his touch evoked. She didn't want him to go.

But he had to do his job. And if he found Jordie…

She lifted one hand and placed it over his, grateful for his tenderness. "Please be careful, Ryder."

He nodded, eyes dark with the memories of their night together as well. "I will." He dropped a kiss on her lips, then gathered his jeans and yanked them on along with his socks and boots.

She watched him dress, silently willing him to

come back to bed and make love to her again. But she bit back the words.

Finding her son was more important. She wanted him back in her arms so they could start their life together.

Her heart squeezed. Only Ryder wouldn't be part of that life.

RYDER PHONED LAW enforcement in Cheyenne, explained the situation and requested backup. A detective named Clay Shumaker met him near the airport.

Ryder checked with the motel clerk, who claimed a woman had signed herself in as Mrs. Jerome Powell.

Ryder showed him a picture of Judy Kinley and he identified her as the woman. Finally they were catching a break.

He and Shumaker approached the room with caution. Shumaker circled to the back to cover the bathroom window in case the couple tried to escape.

Ryder knocked on the door. "FBI. Open up, Blotter. Ms. Kinley. It's over."

The curtain slid aside and two eyes peered out. Judy Kinley.

"Give it up and no one will get hurt," Ryder shouted.

But the door opened and a gunshot rang out. Ryder cursed and jumped behind the rail to dodge the bullet. Blotter raced out, gun aimed and firing.

Ryder raised his weapon and fired back, catching Blotter in the shoulder. Blotter twisted and fired at Ryder.

Ryder's body bounced back as the bullet skimmed his arm.

Chapter Twenty-Five

His arm stung, but the bullet had only grazed him.

Another one skimmed by Ryder's head, missing him by a fraction of an inch. Ryder cursed and released another round, this time sending Blotter to his knees with a gunshot to the belly.

"He's down!" Ryder shouted to the detective.

Shumaker appeared, pushing Judy in front of him, her hands cuffed. She was crying. "Richard!"

Ryder kicked Blotter's gun aside and knelt to check his wounds. Blood oozed from his abdomen, and he'd lapsed into unconsciousness. Dammit.

He wanted Blotter alive and talking.

Ryder called for an ambulance then confronted Judy at the police car. Fear and panic flared in the woman's eyes. "Where is Tia's son?"

"I don't know," Judy said.

"Don't lie to me, Judy. You pretended to be Tia's friend, then you unlocked that window for your brother to come in and kidnap the baby. Why?"

Judy closed her eyes and released a pained sigh. "Money. Richard…he needed it. The people he owed threatened to kill him if he didn't pay up. I…told him I'd help this once, but that was it."

"So you and Richard conspired to kidnap Tia's baby, then sold the child for cash," Ryder said, not bothering to hide the derision in his voice.

"It wasn't like that. That lawyer convinced me that the baby would be better off with two loving parents."

"That wasn't his or your decision," Ryder said.

"Tia loves her son and would be—will be—a wonderful mother."

Judy hung her head in shame.

"Who did he give the baby to?" Ryder pressed.

"I told you, I don't know," Judy said.

"Nothing? Didn't your brother tell you a name or where the couple was from?"

Judy shook her head. "He said it would be better if I didn't know."

Then she wouldn't be culpable. But that was a lie. She was an accomplice to a felony.

The siren wailed, lights flashing as the ambulance arrived. Ryder gestured to the detective. "Book her."

"Please don't let my brother die," Judy said as the detective guided her into the back of his car.

Ryder didn't respond. He told the medics he'd follow them to the hospital.

As soon as Blotter regained conscious, he was going to talk.

He followed the ambulance to the hospital then stayed with the man in the ER.

"He needs surgery," the doctor told him.

"Make sure he survives," Ryder said. "That man kidnapped a child. I want to talk to him."

The doctor scowled. "I understand."

Ryder went to the vending machine for coffee then phoned Gwen for an update. "Please tell me you found something on Frost's computer or in his files."

"We've collected information on at least half a dozen adoptions that might be in question and are assigning a task force to investigate them individually."

"What about a couple who got Jordie Jeffries? An address where he might be?"

"I'm afraid not. We won't give up, though, Ryder."

He closed his eyes in frustration, then returned to the waiting room to pace while he waited on Blotter to get through surgery.

A SOFT KNOCK at the door woke Tia. She stirred and stretched, then realized that it might be Ryder returning.

Maybe with news.

She pulled on her robe and knotted it at the waist, then hurried into the living room. Morning sunlight spilled through the front sheers and warmed the floor against her bare feet.

She hesitated at the door. “Ryder?”

“Yeah, open up, Tia.”

Tia jerked the door open, her heart in her throat. Ryder faced her but stepped aside. “There’s someone here who wants to see you.”

A slender twentysomething woman was stooped down beside a baby carrier. A baby carrier holding a small blue bundle.

Tia gasped and dropped to her knees in front of the baby. “Jordie?”

Ryder cleared his throat. “Yes, it’s him, Tia. He’s fine.”

Tia’s gaze met the young woman’s and she scooped her son up into her arms, tears spilling over. "Oh, my Jordie, I thought I would never see you again." She kissed and hugged him, then held him away from her to soak in his features before she planted more frantic kisses all over his face and head. "Oh, baby, I've missed you so much."

His little chubby face looked up at her, a tiny smile pulling at his mouth. "I love you so much, Jordie." She glanced at Ryder. "How did you find him?"

"Blotter was shot but he regained consciousness long enough to tell me the name of the adopted party."

He gestured toward the woman. "This is Hilary Pickens."

Hilary sniffed and dabbed at her eyes. She was shaking and looked terrified and sad at the same time. "I'm sorry… I didn't know." The woman's voice cracked on a sob and she touched the baby's head lovingly. "I didn't know he was stolen. The lawyer told us that he was ours, that his mother didn't want him."

A myriad of emotions flooded Tia. Rage at the people who'd done this.

Compassion for this woman, whom she believed had been a victim just as she had.

"I took good care of him, I swear," the woman said. "I wanted a baby so badly, and when he came to us, I couldn't believe it finally happened."

"You went through Frank Frost?"

The woman nodded, tears streaming down her face. "But then I saw you on the news and…at first I ran. I thought I couldn't give him back." She gulped a sob. "But then I kept thinking about you and hearing your voice begging to have him home, and I looked into his eyes and knew I couldn't keep him. That it would be a lie, that he wasn't really mine." She glanced at Ryder. "I was packing his things to bring him here when Agent Banks showed up at my door."

Ryder nodded in confirmation.

Tia cuddled Jordie closer, then reached out and took the woman's hand and led her inside.

Then she and Hilary hugged and rocked Jordie together while both of them cried.

RYDER STOOD ASIDE as Tia and the young woman cooed over the baby. He had never met anyone like Tia.

She had suffered while her son was missing, yet she'd accepted the woman who had her child into her home and forgiven her within seconds.

The other woman was suffering, too, he realized. She had wanted a child, but she'd done the right thing when she discovered Jordie had been stolen from his mother without the mother's consent.

His own mother's face taunted him. The pain in Myra's eyes when he'd shown her his birth mother's letters.

He had been hard on her. Had walked away.

He had to see her.

Knowing Tia would be fine now she had her son, he slipped out the back door. She no longer needed him. She had her family.

It was time he reconciled with his own.

Anxiety knotted his gut as he drove to his mother's house. He knocked on the door, childhood memories bombarding him.

The times he was sick and his mother nursed him back to health with her homemade chicken soup and tenderness. The bedtime stories and holidays baking cookies together. His father teaching him to ride a bike and a horse.

The door opened, and his mother appeared, her face pale, eyes serious and worried. "Ryder?"

He offered her a smile. "Mom, I…I'm home."

A world of relief echoed in her breathy sigh, and she pulled him into her arms and hugged him.

Ryder hugged her in return. Nothing could change the way he'd come to be in this woman's life, or the fact that his birth mother had loved him and suffered when he was taken.

But Myra Banks was family, and he loved her.

Three days later

IT WAS TIME he met the rest of his family—the McCullens.

Nerves crawled up Ryder's back as he drove to Horseshoe Creek.

He had tied up the case. With Gwen's help and the task force in place, they had found three more cases in Frost's files of unlawful removal of a child from its birth parent, all three teenagers he had coerced into handing their babies over to him for placement. However, the young women had not been blessed with the hefty payment Frost received—he had kept that for himself.

The mother of the baby Bonnie Cone had adopted agreed to leave her with Bonnie, although Bonnie encouraged the teen to be part of the child's life. Tia's Crossroads program stepped in to facilitate the arrangement.

Tia did not press charges against Hilary, but Hilary joined Crossroads. Helping other families was filling the void left by her own loss, and she'd decided to become a foster parent.

Tia's kindness and Crossroads program were a blessing to so many.

He had been blessed to have met her.

Rich farmland, pastures and stables drew his eye as he wound down the drive to the main farmhouse on Horseshoe Creek. Cash had asked all the McCullens to join him at the house for the meeting.

God. Ryder was so accustomed to being alone, he wasn't sure how to handle this.

Although being alone had its downside. He missed Tia, dammit.

The beauty of the land reminded him that this property had belonged to his birth parents, that they had worked the land and animals and built a legacy for their sons.

And that he was one of them.

It was still difficult to wrap his head around that fact.

The sight of trucks and SUVs at the rambling

farmhouse made his pulse clamor. They were all here waiting to meet him.

What if he didn't fit?

Dammit, Ryder, you're an FBI agent. You've faced notorious criminals. This is family.

Except he felt like a stranger—an outsider—as he parked and walked up to the door.

Before he could knock, Cash met him outside. "Hey, man, glad you came."

Ryder shook his twin's hand, an immediate connection forming. He was no longer alone.

Cash had been out there all along.

Cash looked slightly shaken as well. "The others are waiting."

Ryder nodded, his voice too thick to speak. He'd done his research, knew all the names and faces.

But he wasn't prepared for the warm welcome.

"I'm Maddox, the oldest," the man in the sheriff's uniform said. "Welcome to Horseshoe Creek." He gestured for him to follow. "Everyone is out back on the lawn. Mama Mary fixed a big dinner. We thought we'd do it picnic style."

Cash gave him a brotherly pat on the back, and Ryder shot him a thank-you look, then he walked through the house to the back porch and onto a lush lawn with picnic tables and food galore.

A chubby woman with a big smile and wearing an apron greeted him first. "I'm Mama Mary," she said with a booming laugh. "Nice to finally have all the family here together."

Cash had told him about the bighearted woman who had served as mother to the McCullen boys after Grace was murdered.

She swept him into a hug and he patted her back, emotions thrumming through him when she released him and his brothers lined up to meet him.

TIA HUMMED A lullaby to Jordie as she rocked him, the warmth of his little body next to hers so wonderful that she didn't want to put him in his bed. Each time she did, she feared she'd wake up and find him gone again.

Since his return, she'd had a security system installed, along with new locks. He had been sleeping in the cradle in her bedroom, but one day he would outgrow it and she'd need to move him to the crib.

Still, for now, she clung to him. Listening to his breathing at night gave her peace. His little movements and smiles filled her with such joy that she thought she would burst from happiness.

Except…she missed Ryder.

Her bed seemed big and lonely without him. His scent lingered on the pillow. Images of his naked body tormented her. And when she closed her eyes, she imagined Ryder beside her, holding her, loving her, his big body there to protect her.

But…she hadn't heard a word from him. He'd brought her baby back to her as he'd promised, then disappeared.

Probably onto another case.

He didn't need her or a ready-made family.

She tucked Jordie into the cradle and stroked her thumb over his baby soft cheek. "I love you, little man. Mommy will always take care of you."

She had to be both a mother and father for her son. Somehow she'd find the strength to raise him alone.

And to forget Ryder.

Chapter Twenty-Six

One week later

Ryder parked his SUV on a lush stretch of Horseshoe Creek and studied the pastures, the horses galloping along the hill and the open spaces and imagined a log home built on the property. A swing set out back. A screened porch overlooking the pond.

Family dinners and picnics.

He had tried to stay away from Tia. She needed time to settle with her son. Time to recover from the trauma.

He had helped her on the case, but he wanted

more. But he didn't want to play on the fact that she might feel indebted to him.

His feelings for her had nothing to do with debt.

He'd fallen in love with her, with her kindness and compassion, with her strength, with the way she loved her son and helped others.

But what did he have to offer?

He was a loner who worked a dangerous job. What kind of father would he be?

He wanted to be like Joe McCullen.

The past week he'd spent hours visiting and getting to know the family. They'd taken him in as if he'd always been part of them. He'd also gotten to know Deputy Roan Whitefeather, who turned out to be his half brother. The McCullens had even welcomed Myra into the fold.

He studied the piece of ranch land they'd given him to build on with emotion in his throat. He had a home here if he wanted it.

He did want it. But he didn't want it alone.

What are you going to do about it?

Damn. He swung the SUV around and headed toward Tia's, even though doubts filled him as he left the ranch. Tia had been burned by so many people. She'd admitted she didn't trust anyone. Darren had betrayed and hurt her.

What if she didn't want him?

TIA FINISHED HER morning coffee as she read Jordie a story. Granted, he was too young to really understand, but he seemed to like the sound of her voice.

The doorbell buzzed just as she laid him in the crib. She hurried to the door, brushing her hair into place as she went, then peeked through the window.

Ryder's SUV.

The fear she'd lived with when Jordie was missing returned, yet she reminded herself he was safe now. Richard Blotter and Judy were in jail. Frost had died.

Her son was home and no one would take him from her again.

She took a deep breath and opened the door. Ryder stood in front of her, looking big and tough and so handsome that her lungs literally squeezed for air again.

"Tia?"

His face looked so strained that fear returned. "Is something wrong?"

He shook his head. "No. Can I come in?"

She swept her arm in a wide arc. "Of course."

"How are you and Jordie doing?" he asked.

She glanced toward the nursery door. "Good. I…still get nervous sometimes when I put him in his room, but I have a security system now and baby monitors everywhere."

He nodded, his body rigid. Finally he released a breath. "Would you and Jordie like to take a ride with me?"

She rubbed at her temple. "A ride?"

"Yes, I have something to show you." His dark gaze softened. "Trust me."

She did, with every fiber of her being. "All

right, I'll get him. But you'll have to put my car seat in your SUV, or we can take my minivan."

"I've got it covered."

He had a car seat?

She didn't ask questions, though. She went and scooped Jordie up, then wrapped him in his blanket. Ryder brushed his finger over Jordie's head, his expression tender.

"He's growing."

"I know," Tia said, proud that the ordeal hadn't stunted him.

They walked outside together and he opened the back door for her to settle her baby in the infant seat.

"Does he mind car rides?"

"He sleeps through everything," she said with a smile. She was the nervous one.

Ryder seemed stiff and uneasy, but he slowly relaxed as he drove. She studied the farmland as they left town, then was surprised when they reached a sign that read Horseshoe Creek.

"You met the McCullens?" she asked.

"Yes," Ryder said, his voice gruff. "I've spent a lot of time with the family this past week. They took me in like I was part of them."

"You are part of them," Tia said, sensing the pain that he'd felt and how difficult it was for him to accept the change in his life.

"They even welcomed Myra, my mother," Ryder continued.

"I'm happy for you, Ryder." She leaned her head on her hand. "Family is everything." She still missed her mother and father and brother and wished they were alive to see her son.

Emotions glittered in his dark eyes as he met her gaze. Then he turned down a drive and wound past several stables. Finally he parked at a stretch of land by a pond.

He cut the engine and angled himself to face her. "This is beautiful, Ryder."

A broad smile curved his serious face. "It's mine."

Tia gasped. "Yours?"

"Apparently Joe McCullen left the ranch to all his sons."

"I'm so happy for you. Do you plan to build a house and live here?"

He lifted her hand in his. "Yes. I thought a big farmhouse with a porch with rockers on it." He pointed toward the left side. "A play yard with a swing set could go right there."

Tia's heart began to race. "A swing set?"

He nodded. "And there's a lot of room to ride bikes and horses, and we could teach Jordie to fish one day."

Her breath caught. "Ryder?"

He squeezed her hand, then pressed a kiss to her palm. "I don't just want a house, Tia. I want to build a home here, and I want you and Jordie to be part of it."

"You do?"

"Yes. I love you, Tia." He dug in his pocket and lifted the gold bands they'd worn during their disguise. "I like the feel of this on my hand. I thought we might make it real." He shrugged.

"Of course we can get new ones. A diamond for you if you want."

She'd seen the discomfort on his face when she'd handed him the rings that day. But now… now he seemed relaxed. Happy.

Sincere.

"You aren't doing this just so Jordie will have a father?"

He shook his head. "I want to be his father, if you'll let me." He kissed her fingers one by one. "But I miss you and love you, Tia. I want us to build a life together. To be a family."

Tears welled in Tia's eyes. Happy tears this time.

She gently brushed her hand against his cheek and Ryder swept her in his arms and covered her mouth with his. The kiss was deep, passionate, sensual, filled with promises and yearning.

"Is that a yes?" he murmured.

She nodded and kissed him again. "Yes, Ryder, I love you, too."

She didn't need diamonds. She had her son back. And with Ryder and the McCullens, she would have the big family she'd always wanted.

Epilogue

Six months later

Tia's heart overflowed with love as the reverend announced she and Ryder were husband and wife.

Ryder kissed her thoroughly, the passion between them building. But that would have to wait.

Their family was watching now.

"Later," Ryder whispered against her neck.

She gently touched his cheek. She would never grow tired of touching him. Or hearing his voice. Or looking into his impossibly sexy eyes.

She certainly wouldn't get tired of loving him. "That's a promise."

He gathered her hand in his and they turned to face the guests. Mama Mary smiled from the front row. Just last month she'd married the foreman of the ranch. But she still held the family together with her big warm hugs and comforting food and motherly love.

Maddox, Brett, Ray, Roan and Cash had bonded with Ryder and helped build the house she and Ryder were moving into, while their wives had helped Tia organize the wedding on the lawn.

Cheers and clapping erupted, shouts of joy and happiness and congratulations as she and Ryder stepped from the gazebo to accept glasses of champagne.

She looked across the beautiful ranch and the wonderful McCullens, grateful for their boisterous chaos.

Rose jiggled her baby boy, Maddox's son, Joe, in the stroller while Ryder's mother, Myra, nestled Jordie to her. Willow and Brett's son, Sam, was chasing fireflies with Cash and BJ's adopted boys, Tyler and Drew.

Maddox lifted a champagne flute. "Let's toast to the last McCullen."

Ryder laughed and so did everyone else.

"Hell, he's not the last." Brett touched Willow's bulging belly. "We're just getting started."

"So are we," Ray said as he pulled a pregnant Scarlet against him.

Megan, Roan's wife, smiled sheepishly. "So are we," Roan admitted with an affectionate hug to his wife.

Ryder and Tia exchanged a secretive look. They planned to have more children as well and so did Cash and BJ, but Ryder vowed not to push Tia. Jordie was only a few months old.

Still, as she sipped her champagne and nuzzled his neck, love and passion exploded inside him. Tia wanted at least four, maybe six kids.

Tonight might not be too soon to start.

* * * * *